TO HURT THEM

A LAKE DISTRICT THRILLER

DI SAM COBBS
BOOK 17

M A COMLEY

For Mum,
my guiding star, my greatest cheerleader, and the truest friend I've ever known.
I'll love you for the rest of my days and miss you every second longer.
And for Dex,
my brave, loyal boy — thank you for staying by her side when I couldn't breathe.
You were my strength when I had none.
This book is for both of you.
Love always.

To Mary, gone too soon but never forgotten.

ACKNOWLEDGMENTS

Special thanks as always go to @studioenp for their superb cover design expertise.

My heartfelt thanks go to my wonderful editor Emmy, my proofreaders Joseph and Barbara for spotting all the lingering nits.

A special shoutout to all my wonderful ARC Group, who help to keep me sane.

PROLOGUE

Two months earlier

TRUTH BE TOLD, Max Keane wasn't exactly living up to his name at the moment. He wasn't overly keen on starting a new novel, despite his publisher and agent pestering him, bombarding him with emails and reminding him of his commitments every week. He had what was known in the trade as writer's block, something he'd never had to deal with before in his thirty years of putting pen to paper and, more recently, fingers on the keyboard. It was an unknown quantity that he just couldn't fathom how to overcome.

The more he considered the reason behind his debilitating status, the less he knew how to rectify it. His last book had been a bestseller, as usual. He'd been proud of his achievement in getting to the top of the charts with his tenth book in a row. His audience was growing, especially locally. Sometimes, he appreciated it; at other times, he didn't. That's the reason he had become more reclusive than normal. Writers were notoriously antisocial in the main, but it seemed the more momentum his books gained with every new release, the more he retreated into his shell.

Maybe age had something to do with it. He wasn't really sure what the exact reason was, but sometimes, he found himself procrastinating a lot instead of sitting at his desk, writing scenes for his new masterpiece.

He went through to the kitchen of his small cottage, situated on the edge of the lake. The view alone was usually all the inspiration he needed to get on the right track but, unfortunately, even that was failing him these days. "Hello, Pepsi. What's wrong? It surely can't be time for your dinner already, can it?" He stroked his elderly cat as she stood, rubbing herself against his leg while he waited for the kettle to boil. It was then that he noticed the time on the clock. It was already four-thirty, and he hadn't written a damn word since nine that morning. "Wow, what is sodding wrong with me? Maybe I should just jack it all in. Throw in the towel and retire. But then, what would I do with my time? There's only a certain amount of pottering I can do in our tiny garden. I suppose I could consider rescuing a little dog and take up walking again. How would you feel about that, Pepsi? Having another creature in the house, challenging you for my attention?"

She gave him the answer he needed by turning her back on him and walking over to the back door.

He chuckled and opened it to let her out. "I'm sorry. It was a foolish idea. Will you ever forgive me?"

Pepsi left the kitchen and ran up the crooked path to the bottom of the garden without looking back at him. He left the door ajar, the way he always did when she was in the garden. That way, she'd push it open and gain easy access.

He loved the fact that there were no nearby neighbours, ready to poke their noses into his business. The cottage's location and the fact that it was isolated had been the main reasons he'd bought it over twenty years ago. He always attributed his success as a writer to his ability to cut himself off from civilisation. When he was in the zone, he sat and wrote all day and every day until the first draft of a novel was finished. That could take weeks or months, depending on how well the characters formed in his mind and where the story led them throughout the novel. He was a planner, not a write-by-the-seat-of-your-pants kind of storyteller. Invariably, once his characters found their voice during a draft, the story would veer off somewhere around the halfway point. Damn characters always seemed to know better than he did what makes a bestseller, especially these days.

Recently, he'd downloaded two thrillers from the top of the charts and shaken his head at how distressingly inept they were. Some were written by authors who had topped the charts with their first book but, judging by the reviews he'd read, had failed to recapture the essence of that success in their woeful follow-ups. He strived to be better than them. Which was probably why he wasn't having much luck sitting in the chair and letting himself get immersed in the story that he had spent the last couple of weeks planning out. He knew that all he had to do was write the first page and the story would start to flow. He just didn't have it in him to find the initial words to allow that to happen.

Max made himself a strong coffee and returned to the lounge. He had a designated study where he could work, but he usually found the view from the lounge window exceptional at this time of the year. As spring gave way to summer, the sun enveloped the hills, enhancing their magnificence and ultimately holding him in awe.

He sat at his desk in the bay window and opened his laptop. As he sipped at his drink, the blank page taunted him. Even flicking through his notes failed to prompt him into action.

A noise sounded in the kitchen. Seconds later, Pepsi came sauntering through the door and jumped up on the sofa in her usual spot, where the sun streamed through the curtains. Sadly, that wasn't today. No, there was no sun to entice either of them today.

Another noise sounded in the kitchen. Pepsi looked back over her shoulder and then glanced his way, as if to say, 'Not guilty'.

Max went to investigate, thinking it might be the stray tom that pestered Pepsi now and again. Two masked figures pounced on him before he could react.

"Get back, old man," an automated voice ordered.

Shit! What do I do now? What do they want with me? I hope they don't hurt me and Pepsi. She's all I've got.

He stumbled backwards, bumping into the dresser in the lounge. With his hands raised in front of him, he pleaded, "Please, what are you doing here? What do you want from me?"

"Get his chair, and we'll tie him to it," the shorter of the two intruders ordered.

"What? No, you don't have to do that. Please, I haven't got anything of value in this house. I live a simple life."

"As a bestselling crime novelist?" the shorter person shouted in his face. "That's bollocks. You must have a stash of cash around here somewhere. Don't try to mess with us because there will only be one outcome if you do. Got that, Mr Bestselling author?"

"My name is Max," he corrected the person.

"Whatever. I couldn't give a toss if you were the frigging King of England, we'd still be treating you the same. Where's the money kept?"

He was terrified, enough to make his teeth chatter. "I haven't got any. All my money is sitting either in the bank or in my investments." He winced after realising he had divulged too much information. A blow to the stomach shut him up. "Please, you have to believe me."

"Do we now? Believe a writer who makes a living from making up stupid stories? Why should we? Where's the safe?"

"For the last time, I don't have one. Please, you'll find nothing of value here. Look around you. Most of my furniture is over twenty years old. I'm a recluse. I barely leave my house, only when necessity forces me to."

"We know who and what you are," the taller person said. "We should tie him up and leave him to die."

Their accomplice nodded and agreed, "You're right. We'll do that. We'll tie him to the chair and let him waste away. The cat is quite cute, though. We should take her with us. She'd be better off with someone else."

"No, don't take Pepsi. She's all I've got. She's my little companion. I'd be lost without her in my life."

"You won't have a *life*, so that statement is pretty ridiculous, isn't it? By the time we've finished with you, you'll wish you were dead. We're going to make you suffer, do unthinkable things to you and leave you here to die, bleeding to death," the shorter one said, tipping back their head to laugh.

He couldn't help it; he shuddered under their gaze. With no prospect of getting out of the situation alive, he darted towards the kitchen but was pounced on before he got three feet away from them. A thump in the back sent him tumbling. Max sat on the floor, staring up at the two masked intruders.

He pleaded one last time. "Please, I don't have any money here. Allow me to drive to the bank and get the funds for you. I promise I won't go to the police."

"Is that what one of your characters would say? Would they plead for their life the way you are right now?" the taller one asked.

"Who gives a shit?" The shorter of the two dug the other in the ribs. "Stop getting into a conversation with him. He's getting on my nerves now. Let's get him tied up, do what we've got to do and get the hell out of here."

One of them dragged his office chair into the centre of the lounge. Max was thrust into it. The taller one dipped their hand into the bag next to them and removed a thick rope, which was then tied around Max's chest, restraining him. "Don't do this, please."

"Too late, Max. It's already done. I'm going to gather the things we need," the shorter one said and left the room.

Confused, Max watched the other person go to his desk and rummage through the drawers.

Pepsi observed the stranger with curiosity as they rooted around in Max's personal space. He prayed his beloved cat wouldn't be tempted to do anything foolish that would put her in harm's way.

After several minutes passed, the other person returned to the lounge. "I found these." They held up a carrier bag, the contents of which seemed small as the bag wasn't bulging.

What could they be after, if not money? What stuff are they going to take and, more to the point, what are they intending to do with me? I'm scared. I don't know what to say or do to get out of this. If I remain quiet, they might think twice about hurting me. Yes, I think that's the way to go. I'll button it and hope they take what they want and leave.

"Right, I've got a few bits and pieces here we can add to the mix." The taller intruder added several items to the bag. Max's glasses, which he needed for long distances, were sitting on his desk, so he couldn't make out what the items were. "What about him?"

"We'll deal with him in a moment and then make our move. I'm disappointed there's no money around. I checked his office and couldn't find a safe in there."

"Maybe he's got a wallet on him. Have you?" the taller one asked.

"Yes, but I don't keep any cash on me, not these days," Max replied, his mouth drying up because of the big fat lie he'd just told.

The shorter one stared at Max through narrowed eyes. "We'll see about that."

The person stomped towards him and roughly snatched the wallet from his back pocket. Max closed his eyes, dreading what their reaction was going to be when they discovered he'd been lying.

"There! I knew you were bullshitting us. You old gits think you can get the better of us youngsters, don't you?"

Max opened his mouth to speak, but the person slapped him around the face. His neck jolted with the force. He grunted and gingerly returned his head to its normal position and looked up at the intruder. "I'm sorry," he spluttered, scared shitless by now. "I don't know what came over me."

Another slap sent his head twisting in the opposite direction.

"Stop it. He doesn't deserve that," the taller one said, changing their tune.

The shorter one raised their hand to strike Max a third time, but their associate ran towards them and shoved their accomplice.

"What did you do that for?"

"I said leave him. We've got what we came for. We should go now."

A surge of relief swept through Max; however, it was over in a flash as the shorter one raised a hand and struck him before their mate could stop them.

"I'm out of here. Do what you want to him. I want no part of it."

"Wait, you can't tell me what to do. It was my idea to come here," the shorter one objected.

The other one threw their hand up in the air and marched out of the room. "I'll be in the car. Don't be long."

"That's got rid of my friend. Now, that leaves you and me... alone. What do you propose I should do with you?"

"I don't want any trouble. Please leave me alone. You've got what you came for; you told your friend that. Leave now, and I won't say anything to the police, I promise."

"And if I don't leave now? What if I haven't finished playing with you? What if I have something far more sinister planned for you? What then?"

"I don't know what you want me to say. You've tied me up. If you leave me here, I'll probably die anyway."

"Hmm... that would solve a lot of problems, wouldn't it? You deserve this, Max."

He studied the person, then asked, "What have I ever done to you? I don't know you. Have the courage to show yourself or at least tell me how I've wronged you. Tell me how I can make amends. I'd willingly work with you if that's what you want."

"I don't. I pity you. I despise you for what you've done to my family."

Max frowned and shook his head. "I have no idea what you're referring to. How can I correct things if you won't tell me what it is that I'm supposed to have done wrong?"

The intruder grabbed a chunk of Max's thinning grey hair and yanked his head back. They stared at each other for what seemed like an eternity before the person jabbed him in the stomach with their flattened hand.

"Ugh... please, don't hurt me. Leave now and this will never be mentioned again."

The person spat in his face and left the house. Pepsi growled and hissed at them as they left the room. "You're lucky I don't strangle that cat of yours. Maybe it's not so cute after all. It'll keep until next time, old man. And believe me, there will be a next time."

Max suppressed his excitement at their departure, in case they were deliberately luring him into a false sense of security. After a few seconds, the roar of an engine sounded, and a vehicle sped away from his usually safe retreat. Now, all he had to do was try to get out of his confines. He wiggled so hard that, eventually, the momentum he had built up tipped the chair over on its side.

"Damn, you've never been the sharpest tool in the toolbox, have you? Now look what you've done. How the heck am I going to get out of this?"

Two days later, Eva, his cleaner, let herself in. Pepsi greeted her at the front door, the way she always did. Eva called out his name.

"Oh, thank God. Eva! Eva! I'm in here, in the lounge. Please help me," Max called out, although he didn't know how, as his mouth was as dry as the bottom of a budgie's cage. He fought hard to overcome the embarrassment of having soiled himself.

His cleaner ran into the lounge and gasped when she saw him. "Oh my. Mr Keane, are you all right?"

"No, I'm not. I can't get up. Can you help me?"

Eva was from the Ukraine. She was a slight woman in her fifties who had relocated to the UK during the war with Russia. She tried to right him, but she was unable to shift his dead weight. "I can't do it. Why can't I?"

"It doesn't matter. Can you get a knife from the kitchen? You're going to have to cut the rope to set me free. Either that, or call someone, one of your friends perhaps, for help. Yes, do that. Can you?"

"I don't know many people in the area. All my friends are at work now. I'm sorry. Can I call one of your friends? What about Mr Lawler, the handyman?"

"Yes, yes, yes. That's an excellent idea. Look in the drawer in my desk. You'll find my address book in there."

Eva raced across the room and searched both drawers but couldn't find the address book. She returned to deliver the bad news.

"But it has to be there. Shit! The intruders must have taken it... but why? Never mind, we'll stick with plan A. Can you get the sharpest knife from the kitchen? You're going to have to slice through the rope."

"Yes, I'll do that. Stay there, I'll be right back."

"I assure you, I'm not going anywhere, not anytime soon."

"Ah, sorry."

She ran into the kitchen and returned a few seconds later with his carving knife. He couldn't remember the last time he'd sharpened any of his knives and doubted if any of them would be sharp enough for what was needed.

"Yes, try it. Please, hurry, Eva."

"I try."

She did her best, but the blunt blade had little to no impact on the thick rope. Eva started crying. "I can't do it. I'm such a failure. I want to help you..."

"Don't give up. I've got another idea. Have you got your lighter with you?"

She stopped crying and eagerly nodded. "Yes, it's here in my pocket." She removed a disposable lighter and held it up to check the contents in the light streaming in from the window. "There might not be enough."

"All you can do is try. Wait, I think there's one in the kitchen drawer. Get that one as well."

Eva sprinted into the kitchen. He could hear the drawers being wrenched open and her quickly tossing things aside as she searched for the lighter. She shouted something in her native language and returned to the lounge.

"I've got it."

"That's excellent. Now all you have to do is hold the lighters under the rope."

"But what if I burn you?"

"Just do it. Have faith in your abilities, dear lady. I'm desperate to get up. I don't care if I end up with a few burns. They'll heal in time."

Tears dripped onto her cheeks as she held the flame close to the rope. It took a while for the flame to make an impression on his bindings, but then, much to his dismay, one of the lighters ran out of fluid.

"Shit!" Eva muttered.

"Don't worry. Just do your best. Don't give up."

"I'll try again. Here goes."

After several minutes, Max tried tugging on the cord around his chest as the intruders had failed to bind his hands. It creaked a little. He tugged harder, and eventually the rope fell away. The relief in them was palpable. Eva stood and held out a hand to assist him to his feet. He slipped his hand into hers, but between them, they failed to get him upright. He released his grip and caught his breath before he attempted something different. Max flipped onto his knees, then pushed against the chair, forcing himself up onto his feet. Eva supported him, and it wasn't long before he was standing upright with Pepsi winding herself around his legs.

Eva waved her hand at the cat. "Shoo now, Pepsi. Let him move."

"She'll be hungry. Neither of us has eaten for a couple of days."

"You sit. I make you something to eat and fetch you a glass of water." Eva helped him to a chair she fetched from the kitchen and left him there while she prepared him some food. When she came back, she found him at his desk. "What are you doing?" she screeched. "You can't work. You need to rest, Mr Keane. You are not a well man."

"I'm fine. I need to report the crime. I've called the police. They're sending someone out to see me. Thank you so much for your help, Eva."

"I did nothing. Are you sure you're all right? I could ring an ambulance and get someone to check you over."

"That's very kind of you. No, I'm sure I'll be okay." He glanced down at his soiled trousers and apologised. "I'm sorry you had to see me in this state. Please don't think badly of me."

Eva growled and frowned. "Now you're being silly. How long have you been like that?"

"Two days, maybe more. I'm so glad you came and rescued me."

"Me too. Don't worry about the mess. I can help you upstairs, after you've eaten, of course. You need to eat and drink first. That should be your priority. It'll help you gain your strength."

He nodded. "Yes, I will. Thank you." He nibbled on the cheese and tomato sandwich she'd made for him as he glanced out of the window at the wonderful scenery surrounding his once tranquil cottage. His mind was numb. He tried to block out the bizarre thoughts of leaving his tiny home.

I can't leave. I've spent my whole life working to achieve something like this. It's the isolation I love, and yet now, going forward, I believe it might be the one thing I fear most in this life... after what's happened.

He ate and sipped at the tea she had made him until it was all gone. He was expecting an officer to arrive within the hour. "Eva," he called.

His cleaner appeared in the doorway. "Yes, Mr Keane? Have you eaten your food?"

"I have. Can you help me up the stairs now?"

"I can try."

Together, they managed to get him into the bathroom, where Eva ran a shower for him. He thanked her, and she left him to it.

"I'll be in the bedroom, tidying up in there. Give me a shout if you need me."

"I will. I won't be long."

"Take your time. You should have a soak in the bath, really. That would be much better for you."

Max smiled and shook his head. He couldn't think of anything worse than sitting in the tub with the caked-on shit on his backside, loosening and ending up floating in the water around him. No, taking a shower would definitely be the better option.

After showering and feeling a lot fresher, he slipped on the towelling robe, an old one from the back of the door, and walked along the hallway to his bedroom.

"Hi, how do you feel now?" Eva asked.

"Much better. Can I help?"

"No. I'm almost finished. I thought I would change your sheets. I know I changed them last week, but you will need some extra comfort tonight after what has happened to you."

He smiled, appreciative of her thoughtfulness. "You're a treasure." He shooed her out of the room, quickly dressed and then collected his dirty clothes from the bathroom, which he placed into a black bag and flung into the bin outside.

Eva joined him in the kitchen. "You look and smell much better now, no offence." She laughed nervously, clearly unsure if she'd said the right thing or not.

The doorbell rang, and Eva scurried out of the room to answer it. "I get it."

He went through to the lounge and waited for Eva and the officer to appear.

"Hello, Mr Keane. How are you?"

"Much better now I've had a chance to clean up. Would you like a drink?"

"I'll decline, if you don't mind, but thanks for the offer." The officer sat on the sofa and typed up the information on his tablet. "Now there's no rush. In your own time, I'd like you to tell me what happened."

So, that's what Max did for the next ten minutes. He went over every sordid detail of his encounter with the intruders. The officer typed and then repeated all the facts back to him.

"You've been through hell. I'm truly sorry you had to contend with that, sir. Is there anything you can tell me about the two suspects? What about their height for a start?"

"Now you're asking. I was sitting most of the time. It's hard to judge how tall someone is when they're towering over you. They were different heights. One was probably about six feet, and the other was slightly smaller, maybe five-eight or nine."

"What about their builds? Would you say they were slim or stocky?"

"Both very slim. They wore balaclavas. The shorter one had piercing blue eyes."

"Did either of them have a distinctive accent?" the officer asked.

"No, they wore a contraption that altered their voices, not sure what something like that would be called."

"I'll look into it. I believe there are a few tools like that on the market at present. Do you know what they were after? Why they came here specifically?"

"I presumed it was for money. They removed about fifty quid from my wallet. They were disappointed I didn't have a safe with excess money in it. But then, one of them said something strange to me."

The officer tilted his head. "Oh, can you tell me what that was exactly?"

"The person said, 'I despise you for what you've done to my family.' Honestly, to my knowledge, I've never done anything bad to anyone. Definitely nothing that would warrant someone tying me up and leaving me to die."

"Do you believe it might have been a case of mistaken identity?"

"I don't know. Maybe. I went through hell and back when they left. I was stuck on the floor for two days. Thank God, Eva had a key, and she was due to clean today. I dread to think what would have happened to me if I didn't have a cleaner." He shook his head, ridding himself of the image of him starving to death, tied to the chair, and becoming a skeleton in no time. As it was, he had very little meat on his bones.

"And how long has Eva worked for you?"

"About eighteen months. She's a sweetheart. Came over as a refugee from the Ukraine."

The officer noted down the information and looked up to ask his next question. "Can you tell me if anyone has made any threats to you in the past three to six months?"

"No. While I was lying there on the floor," he said, pointing to the exact spot in the middle of the lounge, "I racked my brains, trying to think if I had wronged anyone in my past. I have to tell you that I haven't. At least, I don't believe I have. This is all totally bewildering and nonsensical to me."

"You say they took a bag of items with them. Do you know what they took?"

"No. I couldn't see. The taller one had a good rummage through my desk in the lounge. They picked out several items from the drawers. The shorter one left the room and searched my office. I'm presuming they were initially looking for money."

"I see. Did they go upstairs at all?"

"No, I don't think so. The floorboards creak up there. I think I would have heard them moving around."

The officer flipped the cover over his tablet. "Well, I think that just about covers everything. Are you sure you wouldn't prefer to go to the hospital to get checked over, sir?"

"No. I'm fine. I'm not really one for wasting a doctor's time. The NHS is under enough strain as it is these days."

"You're right. It's not getting any easier for them either. Okay, well, I'll leave you to it. It might be a good idea to get a locksmith in to change your locks, just in case they discovered a spare key during their search."

"I'll get that sorted as soon as I can. Thank you."

"We'll be in touch if we uncover anything. Take care of yourself. Ensure all your doors are locked at all times, day and night."

"Don't worry, I've already thought about that."

"I'll leave you one of my cards. If you should think of anything else that I should know about, don't hesitate to call me. Also, if you work out what the intruders took, that will help the investigation going forward, too."

"I'll have a proper look once you've gone and get back to you. I want to thank you for attending so quickly. It's good to know the police are still reliable in this area."

"We strive to be, sir."

Eva appeared in the doorway. "You stay there, Mr Keane. I will show the officer out."

"Thank you, Eva." He watched them leave the room and expelled a long breath. His heart was racing. He was determined to get it back to normal so inhaled and exhaled a few more breaths.

Eva came back into the room. "He seemed a nice man."

"He did. Let's hope they find the rascals who did this. Damn, I should have asked him if there was a spate of robberies in the area."

"Yes, maybe they were here because they didn't think you would have good security. You need to sort that out, Mr Keane. It's important for you to feel safe in your own home."

"You're right. I'll ring Mr Lawler and get him to come out at his earliest convenience."

"Do you need me for anything else today, sir?"

"No, I don't think so. You've been a gem. Saying thank you doesn't seem enough for what you've done for me today."

Eva smiled. "It's my pleasure. You're a very good man. You've got my number. Call me if you need anything."

"I will. Thanks, Eva."

She left the house, and when she walked out of the front door, he couldn't help but feel lost and out of control. Was this how he was going to live the rest of his life? Apprehensive, on tenterhooks, listening out for strange noises, waiting for someone to attack him? He shuddered at the thought and took up the search for his address book. Once he'd located it, under a pile of papers in his in-tray, he rang the handyman and apprised him of the situation. Jim said he could pop around later that day.

He ended the call with mixed feelings—relieved that Jim could visit him so quickly, but also fearful and nervous about being alone in the house he loved so much; his home that had served him so well when he needed solitude.

1

"Stay there. You're quite safe, for now."

"I can't cling to the edge for long."

"She'll be here soon. I saw a glimpse of her bright-green top coming around the bend over there. That's not too far away. Just hang in there."

"Literally. Are you sure there isn't a better way to surprise her?"

"I'm sure. She won't expect this. Have faith in me."

Another couple of minutes passed before the sound of movement came from below them. She was there, within striking distance. It was time for them to make their move. The shorter one gave their accomplice the thumbs-up. The element of surprise would be just what was needed to take the bitch down. She was athletically built and a fitness instructor in the village. She often came out here for a run, at least two to three times a week.

As Angel passed beneath them, one of the assailants dropped from their hiding place and landed in front of her. The shorter one joined them. Angel saw the balaclavas and tried to run. They each grabbed one of her arms. The taller one slapped some tape over Angel's mouth to prevent her from screaming.

This needed to happen swiftly before another jogger or hiker came along. She struggled to get out of their grip, feistily pulling her arms and kicking out at them. Her muffled cries for help fell on deaf ears, though.

The shorter one got in her face and sneered, "Shut up. No one is going to hear you."

The muffled cries for help still came until the taller one jabbed Angel in the stomach and warned her, "Shut the fuck up, or we'll kill you here."

The partners in crime shared a knowing look and then forced her to the ground. The shorter one removed the flask from their backpack, and their accomplice tore off the tape.

"Drink this."

Angel pursed her lips and refused to drink it. She twisted her head away from them.

"Drink it, or we'll go after your mother."

Confusion clouded her eyes when she studied each of them. "Who are you? What do you want from me?"

"We've told you what we want. Drink it."

The flask was rammed against her lips. The taller one gripped Angel's hair and yanked her head back, while the other forced her mouth open. She gagged on the liquid but swallowed it nonetheless.

"That's a good girl. Now we're all going to sit here peacefully and enjoy the view of the lake while the effects take hold."

"What have you given me?"

"Something to help you sleep. It won't take long now. Bear with us."

Angel's eyes became heavy until she struggled to keep them open. Once they were closed and her pulse had slowed drastically, the shorter one bashed a rock against her head. The blood poured out of the wound.

"We need to lay her down and arrange the body. The police will never guess what has happened to her."

"What about during the post-mortem? They're bound to test the body for extra substances."

"Maybe. We'll see about that. Come on, standing around here discussing what might happen afterwards isn't going to help."

They spent the next few minutes trying out different angles for her legs until the shorter one was satisfied with how the body had been arranged. "There, I think that will do. Let's snap off a few photos. I intend to put them in a scrapbook at the end."

"You're sick. That bloody warped mind of yours is dangerous."

"Don't you forget it either. Right, let's get out of here and back to the car." After checking Angel's pulse for the final time and finding nothing, they removed their masks, shoved them in their backpacks and left a single item at the scene. "That'll keep the police guessing."

They laughed and ran back towards the car park. They passed a lone hiker on the way and cheekily said hello to him.

"Enjoy your walk. Lovely day for it."

"Have you been all the way round?" he asked.

"No, we've just come over the bridge. We walked the flat route today. Decided to walk halfway and back."

"Ah, yes. Okay, I think I'm going to challenge myself this morning and do the complete circuit. I've got enough sandwiches with me to feed an army. I have a caring wife who never lets me go hungry."

"She sounds a gem to me. Have fun," the shorter one said.

The man walked off, and they turned towards the car park.

"That was dumb."

"What was?"

"You, striking up the conversation with that bloke."

"Don't be ridiculous. You worry too much. Get in the car. You can buy me lunch at The Gather."

"Sod off. I haven't got the funds for that. My shifts have been cut at work."

"Jesus, you're hopeless. All right, I'll get this one. You can buy me lunch next week."

"Ain't going to happen. I'm skint for the foreseeable. We should have nicked her purse before we did away with her."

"Maybe you're right. It's too late now, unless you fancy trotting back there."

"Screw you. If I did that, it would put me in the frame for her murder."

The other one grinned. "Stop whining!"

∼

"What's the rush?" Bob asked Sam as she put her foot down on the dual carriageway between Workington and Whitehaven.

"I don't like it when I hear a body has been found at one of the most picturesque places in Cumbria."

"You mean at your favourite lake?"

Sam grinned. "That as well. I don't think Ennerdale Bridge has recovered from the last investigation that hit the village. I chat with Emma regularly, and she told me these days the villagers are wary of newcomers or people passing through."

"Any reason why?" Bob asked, puzzled. "It was a local who was killing off the visitors to the village last time, wasn't it?"

"Yes, that's true. It must have been horrendous for them to deal with, and now we have yet another incident on our hands."

"It's called life. It sucks at times. Correction, actually it's shit most days, especially for me at the moment."

"Oh dear, don't tell me things are rough at home between you and Abigail?"

"All right, I won't. But I'd be lying."

"Oh, mate. Sorry to hear that. If you need a shoulder to cry on, you know I'm always here for you."

"I wouldn't want to bore you with the ins and outs of our humdrum life."

Sam punched him gently in the thigh. "Why don't you go away for the weekend, just the two of you? No distractions, just you two, discussing what's right and wrong about your relationship over a bottle of wine or two."

"Sounds umm... like an evening of torture."

"Uh-oh, you're supposed to say it sounds idyllic and yes, we'd love to jump at the chance to do it."

"Not! We'll sort it out, eventually. You're lucky you don't have kids. They can be a pain in the rear, especially during their teenage years."

"There's a reason some women prefer not to have children. Let's leave it there, shall we? I will say one thing before we end this conversation, though."

"Go on, I'm all ears."

"My advice would be for you not to take it out on Abigail. Most parents I know do better with their kids when they handle things as a united front."

Bob sighed. "And there lies the problem. Abigail and I have very different parenting methods."

"Unless you work on a compromise, then the issue is only going to get worse over time. You do realise that, don't you?"

"Yep. It's already written in stone. Actually, it'll probably be written on my tombstone."

"That's a bit over the top, even for you, Bob."

Sam drove down the narrow road that led to Ennerdale Water. A red squirrel darted across the road in front of her, forcing her to slam on the brakes. "Jesus, I thought we were goners there."

"Damn critters. Is it any wonder their numbers are dropping?"

"Nope, I can't argue with you on that front. Let's try again." Sam continued on the journey to the car park.

An officer on duty lowered the crime scene tape, allowing them to enter, and raised it again after Sam had parked the car. There were three SOCO vans and two extra patrol cars, along with several other vehicles in the immediate area.

Sam got out and shouted over to the officer who had given them access, "Where am I likely to find the crime scene? Is it far?"

"Not too far, ma'am. You might need some decent walking shoes. My partner is down by the lake. He'll show you the way."

"Thanks." Sam opened the boot of her car and changed her shoes, then withdrew a couple of protective suits and two sets of protective shoe covers before she and Bob set off.

As they walked down the track to the lake, with the stunning scenery ahead of them, Sam shook her head. "Why here? Why do killers think they have the right to spoil people's memories of this wondrous location?"

"That's like asking me how killers have the audacity to breathe just like the rest of us."

Sam sighed. "Yeah, I suppose you're right. Look at this place."

"I'm looking," he said, his tone non-committal. "And?"

"Don't you feel it? Doesn't it pull at your heartstrings?"

Bob shrugged. "Sorry, I can't say it does."

"Wow, seriously?"

"People get joy from different things in this life. What impresses you doesn't necessarily do the same for me. Let's not fall out about it."

"I have no intention of falling out with you. Okay, let's drop this topic of conversation and revisit it when you're in a better mood."

"Hey, just for the record, there's nothing wrong with my mood today."

Sam felt it would be best not to respond. They approached the officer on guard by the bridge. Sam flashed her ID. "Is it far?"

"About a quarter of a mile that way, ma'am." He glanced down at her feet. "I was going to suggest wearing appropriate footwear, but I see you've already thought about that."

"I have. I'm a frequent walker up here."

They set off again. Sam led the way through the narrower parts of the track. Most of her journey was spent eyeing the spectacular view of the lake beside them. In the distance, she could see the SOCO crew standing out in their white suits.

"You'll be pleased to know it's not far now."

"Great. I think I've scuffed my shoes enough for one day already."

"Sorry, maybe you should consider carrying a pair of walking shoes or wellies in my car, in the future."

"Perhaps. I'll think about it."

It was another five minutes before they arrived at the crime scene. She surveyed the area. The track was limited, and the cliff was overhanging above them.

"Did she fall?" Sam asked Des Markham, the pathologist, as he walked towards her.

"Possibly. I've not really had the chance to properly assess things yet."

"Who found her?" Sam asked.

He pointed to a man on the other side of the track who was wearing a large rucksack. "Chap called Clive Beaumont."

"Is he okay?"

"He's a bit shaken up. I told him to go back to the car, but he's adamant that he wants to continue on his walk. He believes it will help him clear his head after what he's witnessed. He's eager to get off, so you might want to have a word with him first. That'll give me time to do the necessary around here."

"Will it be okay if we squeeze past? Otherwise, it'll be a seven-mile walk to get to him."

Des tutted. "If you must. We're going to have to form a human chain to allow you to pass. I don't want you getting too close to the body."

"Great," Bob muttered behind her. "More scuffs to look forward to on my bloody shoes."

"Wind your neck in, Grumpy."

The chain was formed close to the water. Sam managed to escape dipping her feet in the lake, but unfortunately, because Bob was wearing his ordinary shoes with no grip, he slipped off the rock and one foot ended up in the water.

"Jesus, remind me again why I do this job."

Sam laughed. "Sorry, mate. You should reconsider my suggestion at the earliest opportunity."

"Why do you always take pleasure in stating the obvious?"

"I wouldn't be me if I didn't. Are you all right?"

"No comment."

They continued along the track until they reached the witness.

"Hello, Mr Beaumont. I'm DI Sam Cobbs, and this is my partner, DS Bob Jones. We won't keep you too long. I know you're keen to get on your way."

"I come here regularly, mostly to clear my head. Never in my wildest dreams did I ever imagine stumbling across a dead body. What's worse is that I know her."

"You do? As in she's a regular here, or do you know her name?"

"She's called Angel Pritchard. She's a fitness coach in the village." He shook his head and glanced over Sam's shoulder at Des and his team.

"I'm sorry this has come as a shock to you. I don't suppose you happen to know her address, do you?"

"No, sorry. The folk at The Gather should be able to point you in the right direction with that information."

"Thanks, we'll visit them after we've finished here. Can you tell me if you saw anyone else around when you arrived? Did you pass anyone along the path, perhaps?"

"Back on the stretch between the bridge and the car park. Actually, it was a member of staff from the café and a friend."

"I see, and were they acting suspicious at all?"

"No, not in the slightest. They told me they'd walked halfway round the lake but had taken the easier route."

"Over the bridge?"

"That's right. I needed to challenge myself today. Well, that was my intention, until I stumbled across Angel. Umm... I'm not sure how to tell you this, but I got close to her. I wanted to see if there was anything I could do to help her. You know, I checked if she was still breathing. I'm a first aider at work. It wouldn't have felt right not trying."

"It's okay. We're going to need to take a DNA sample from you so we can dismiss you from our enquiry."

"I'm sorry. I know how important it is to keep a crime scene clean..." He swallowed and then shook his head as if fighting back the tears.

"Please, there's no need. I would hope anyone in your situation would do the same."

"I can't get over finding her. I suspect she fell from above. I saw the blood on the rock close to her head."

"We'll have to see what conclusions the pathologist and his team reach about things. Okay, I don't want to keep you here longer than is necessary. If you can give me your address and phone number, I'll get an officer to call you to set up a convenient time to take down your statement. We'll also need to take a DNA sample from you, to dismiss you from our investigation."

Bob withdrew his notebook and wrote down the details Clive gave them.

"You're free to continue your walk. Again, I'm sorry you've had to witness this today. Are you going to be okay?"

"I think so."

"Thank you for calling it in. Please take care on your walk."

"I will. Focusing my mind on the path ahead will help me get over what I've had to deal with here, today."

Sam smiled and nodded, although she doubted if his statement would be true.

Clive turned and walked along the narrow path close to the water's edge.

Once he was out of earshot, Bob said, "Rather him than me. Especially carrying that heavy bag on his back."

"I agree. I hope he's going to be all right. The path can get tricky underfoot around the next bend."

"He seems to realise what a challenge the terrain can be."

Sam waved to draw the team's attention, and they formed the human chain once more.

"How's it going?" Sam asked Des once they were back on the path again.

Bob shuffled closer to her to get a firmer footing away from the water.

"Upon close examination, it would appear she fell and cracked her head on the rock beside her," Des confirmed. "Of course, I'll know more once the PM has been performed."

Sam's gaze rose to the slight overhanging above and then to Angel's body.

Something doesn't feel right to me. Why would she climb up there in the first place? Everyone local is aware of the challenges the lake holds without going off the track like that.

She saw something poking out from under the corpse. "What's that?" She pointed at the object.

One of the techs was crouched, taking photos of the body. Des gave him the go-ahead to investigate.

He held it up in his gloved hand. "I think it's a leather bookmark."

Sam frowned. "Could it have slipped out of her backpack when she fell? If she fell?" she added.

"Possibly." Des's gaze drifted upwards. "You know, the more I look at it, the more I'm beginning to question whether she fell or not."

"I was wondering the same," Sam said.

"Why didn't you say something?" he challenged her.

"Because you're the expert, and I thought my assumption was wrong."

He tutted. "If you have a theory, it's always better to share it, Inspector."

"Consider me told. I'll do that in the future."

Des changed positions to check the angle of Angel's limbs once more. "Yes, I can see it now. The body has been moved or put in a position for us to believe she fell. Most people assume that limbs end up twisted after a fall. That simply isn't true. A lot depends on the height of the fall as to how the body lands. The distance from the ledge above wouldn't have given the victim enough time to change position before impact."

Sam nodded, understanding and appreciating his theory. "So, does that mean we're looking at a suspicious death?"

Des raised a finger. "Let's not jump the gun. We'll carry out the necessary tests and get back to you. For now, I'm going to get a pain in the arse from sitting on the fence." He grinned.

"I'm with you. Clive Beaumont told us her name."

"He knew her?" Des appeared shocked to learn the news.

"Yes. She's a regular walker here, but she's also a fitness coach in the village."

His eyes formed tiny slits as he studied the victim once more. "Which kind of adds to the argument, doesn't it? If she was agile, it would be second nature for her to attempt to land on both feet. Why would her legs be twisted like that?"

"Does she have any broken bones?"

"None that I can see. Yes, I'm going with my gut here and saying it as I find it. This has been staged, and I believe the victim was murdered."

"Bashed over the head by the rock?" Bob queried.

"So it would seem. The question you're going to need to find an answer to is, why?"

"Hmm... what do you think the bookmark is about? Was that part of the plan? Has the killer planted it there?"

"It seems plausible," Des admitted.

Sam shook her head, her gaze drifting sideways to the lake and the mountains all around them. "Why here? What possesses someone to take a life in these tranquil surroundings? Sorry, that's twice I've asked that question today. Bob is going to get sick and tired of hearing it."

"You could say that," her partner chipped in.

"Your guess is as good as mine, Inspector," Des replied. "Right, have you seen enough? There are some dark clouds forming overhead. It doesn't take long for the weather to take a turn for the worse when we're this high up."

"Okay, we'll leave you to it. Let me have the PM report as soon as you can, please."

"Of course. Can you make it back okay?"

"Yes, I'll be all right. Not sure if Bob is willing to take the risk, though."

"I might as well go for the double, even things up. No point just having one wet foot when you can have two. I wouldn't want the other one missing out, would I?"

Sam laughed. "You said all of that with such a straight face, too."

He smirked.

"Speak soon, Des. If you discover anything else, can you call me?" Sam led the way back up the path.

"I will. Take care."

Once they were back on firmer ground, she surveyed the area around them and shook her head. "It doesn't seem right, finding a dead body here. Sorry, that's the last time I'm going to say that today. Let's stop off at The Gather and have a chat with Emma and her team."

"Goodie. I missed breakfast this morning because Abigail and I had an argument. One of their bacon and sausage rolls would go down a treat."

"I'll let you off this time. I still maintain it's the best coffee around here, so I'll be diving into one of their flat whites. You can place the order while I have a chat with Emma."

Emma was thrilled to see Sam. She hugged her, then steered her into her office. "It's been ages, too long since we've seen you. What's been happening?"

"Sorry, you're not going to like what I have to tell you."

They both sat down.

"Oh God, don't tell me you're here on official business again."

"Afraid so. Furthermore, the victim is local, and I have a feeling you might know her."

Emma slapped a hand over her mouth but slowly lowered it. "I'm almost too scared to ask... Go on, who is it?"

"Angel Pritchard."

"No, no, no... she's one of my best friends. How? Was she killed in an accident? Forget I asked that. It was a dumb question, considering the cases you deal with on a daily basis."

"Sorry, yes, you're right. She was found up at the lake. Another hiker discovered her body."

Tears welled up and dripped onto Emma's cheeks. She grabbed a tissue from the box on her desk and blew her nose. She plucked another one and wiped her eyes. "She was only in here yesterday. She runs a class once a month from the Community Hall upstairs. She was in here asking if she could extend it to twice a month, as more people in the surrounding villages were interested in taking part. Oh my, I can't believe this. Can you tell me how she died?"

"We're not completely sure. The pathologist will need to perform a post-mortem before he can identify the cause of death. Between you and me, only because I know I can trust you, we believe her body was staged to make it look as though she had fallen from the ledge above and hit her head on a rock."

"What? How dreadful. Oh God, what a bloody world we live in. She was an absolute gem. She meant a lot to this community. The villagers are going to be shocked again when they hear the news. I'm dumbfounded to hear this. Shit! I've just realised..."

"What?"

"Her mother is here at the moment, having coffee with a friend."

Sam closed her eyes momentarily and sucked in a breath. "Was Angel married?"

"No, she had a boyfriend. He lived with her. Christ, this sounds awful, but they were having issues."

"Were they still living together?"

"Yes. Angel tried to kick him out. It was her house, but he was struggling to find somewhere else to live. He's not from the area. They met on a train a couple of years ago. It was a whirlwind romance that fizzled out over the past year or so. It took her months to pluck up the courage to tell him it was over. I feel so bad. I was the one who encouraged her to do it. If he's done this..."

Sam raised a hand. "We can't make assumptions like that, Emma."

"No, I'm sorry. That's the inner amateur sleuth in me coming out. What a waste of time I was on your previous case. Yes, you definitely need to ignore me. Her poor mum. She hasn't long lost her husband, Angel's stepdad. Her father ran off years ago, leaving her mum struggling to bring up Angel on her own. She's got a lot of health problems and walks with a stick. Will you have a word with her now?"

"I might need to take her somewhere discreet. Is the room upstairs available?"

"Shit! No, some of the bosses from Sellafield have booked it for a meeting. It's an all-day job. You can use my office or the room next door."

"That would be perfect. You're a star. Umm... what about upstairs? Have you got any bookings for the rest of the week?"

"Nothing after today. Do you want to use it as a base again?"

"If it comes to it—that is, if you wouldn't mind? It made life so much easier than having to trawl back to the station two or three times a day. We'll need to canvass the area."

"Go for it. You know you're always welcome here. Can I get another hug?"

They both stood, and Sam hugged her tightly.

"We'll find the person responsible, I promise you."

Emma wriggled out of the embrace and wiped her eyes again on another tissue. "Okay, I need to pull myself together. This shouldn't be about me. Saying that, I'm going to miss Angel. She was such a lovely person."

"There's no rush. We can wait a few minutes while the news sinks in, love."

"No. If that were my child you had found, I'd want to know straight away. Come on, I'll introduce you to Maria."

Sam rubbed her arm. "If you're sure?"

Emma nodded a few times, her brow furrowed with perplexity. "Absolutely."

They went back into the café, where Bob was already tucking into his bacon and sausage roll. He waved at her.

"Excuse me while I bring Bob up to date." Sam crossed the room and said, "I won't be long. Stay there, I'm going to have a chat with Angel's mum."

He dropped his roll on the plate. "What? She's here?"

"Yes. Emma is going to make the introductions. I'll take her in the office and break the news. There's nothing you can do for now. Scratch that, you can organise the team for me. Emma's agreed to allow us to use the room upstairs again. Ring Claire when you get the chance and ask her to do whatever is needed to set up a temporary base here from tomorrow. It's in use the rest of the day."

He gathered the contents of his roll together. "Okay, it won't take me long to devour this. Good luck with the mother."

"Thanks."

Emma was standing at the table, speaking with Maria and her friend. Sam walked over with her shoulders back, giving her the confidence she needed to speak with the women.

"Maria, Liz, this is a good friend of mine, Detective Inspector Sam Cobbs."

"Hello, ladies. It's lovely to meet you. Sorry to interrupt you, but Maria, would it be possible to have a quiet chat with you?"

"Me? May I ask why? Sorry, yes, please take a seat."

Sam smiled. "In private, if possible. Emma said it's okay if we use her office."

"But that would be rude of me. Liz and I are having a conversation and…"

Emma squeezed Maria's shoulder. "Go with Sam. She's got something to tell you. I'll get Liz another coffee and keep her company."

Maria's gaze shifted between her friend, Emma, and Sam. "This is most unusual. I don't think it's right to invite a friend out and leave her halfway through a conversation."

Liz seemed to sense there was more to it and placed her hand over Maria's. "It's fine by me. I'll have a catch-up with Emma. Hey, you know me, I'm not one to turn down a free coffee, especially around here."

"I feel awful, but as long as you're okay with it, Liz." Maria collected her walking stick and stood. She followed Sam back to the office; it took longer than she anticipated it would.

"Take a seat, Maria. You have Emma's chair. It'll be more comfortable for you."

"Very well. What's this about? Sam, is it?"

"That's right. We were called out this morning after someone found a body up at the lake."

Maria gasped and immediately shook her head. "No, don't you dare tell me it was my daughter. She was up there this morning."

Sam reached for her hand, but Maria tucked it into her jacket pocket.

"I'm sorry to have to tell you this, but yes, Angel's body was found by a hiker."

Maria screamed. "No! Not my beautiful daughter. There must be some mistake."

Seconds later, Liz wrenched open the door, and Emma was standing behind her. "Maria, was that you? Good heavens, what have you said to her?"

Maria held out her hand for Liz to take.

Her friend rushed past Sam. "Whatever is the matter, dear?"

"It's my Angel. She's gone."

"Gone where, Maria?" Liz asked, confused.

"No, she's de…" Maria tried to tell her then paused to swallow.

Liz fell against the doorframe. "What are you saying? She can't be. I only saw her this morning. She was excited about going on her usual walk up the lake."

Sam laid her hand over Maria's. "My partner and I have just come from up there. Unfortunately, a hiker found Angel's body. He's a local. He told me he recognised her. He tried to help her before he realised she was already dead."

Everyone fell silent. Sam's heart went out to Maria, who was bent over, sobbing so hard she was struggling to breathe properly.

"Oh, Maria, I don't know what to say," Emma said. "It's devastating news. We'll all miss her."

Sam plucked a couple of tissues from the box and handed them to Maria. "Here you are. There's nothing more I can tell you about what happened, not until the pathologist has conducted the post-mortem."

"Oh no, she doesn't have to go through one of them, does she?" Maria cried.

Sam sighed. "I'm sorry. Yes, in instances like this, it's procedure."

"I want to go home." Maria used the stick to assist her to her feet.

Sam glanced up at Liz and Emma, her eyes widened. "Do you have a car here?"

"We came in mine," Liz said. "Come on, love. I'll drive you home."

"Thank you. I'm sorry, Emma, Sam. I can't stay here a moment longer. I need to be on my own."

"I quite understand," Sam said. "I'll drop by and see you in a few days."

"Okay. I don't know what to do in these circumstances. Will someone help me?"

"Nothing right now, not until the pathologist has carried out the post-mortem. Angel's body won't be released until after that. Des Markham, the pathologist, will run through what you should do next when you meet him."

"Thank you. Can we go, Liz?"

"Of course."

"I'll give Sam your phone number and address, Maria. You go home and take it easy. We're all here if you need us. Please remember that."

"Thank you, Emma."

Liz and Maria left the office.

Emma entered the room and threw herself into her chair. "I have no idea how you do that, day in and day out. I mean, having the courage to tell people their loved ones have died."

Sam shrugged. "It's the one part of the job I detest the most. It's never easy. The relatives show their grief in different ways, but it amounts to the same thing. They know they're never going to see their loved ones again. How are you holding up?"

Emma waved her hand. "I'm fine. Don't go worrying about me. I feel for Maria, though, especially after losing her husband last year. Now she'll be burying her daughter as well. None of us expected that, least of all her."

"I know. It's going to be tough on her. I think she'll be relying on you and all the villagers to help her get through it."

"We'll be here for her. We're a strong community in that respect. What happens now?"

"I'll need to speak with her boyfriend, Luke, next. Bob's organising the team for me, if he's finished stuffing his face. I'd better check on him."

"I'll get you a coffee. It's a shame we haven't got a license to sell alcohol. I bet you could do with a stiff one to help you cope with what lies ahead of you."

"I never touch the stuff while I'm on duty. A coffee will suffice, thanks, Emma."

Sam left the office and found her partner talking to one of the young waitresses.

"And then I had this one not long after I'd plucked up the courage to have the first." Bob rolled up his sleeve and showed her one of his ghastly tattoos.

"Do you have to do that here? You're going to put the punters off their food."

The waitress blushed and walked away, mumbling an apology as she went.

"Poor Grace," Bob said. "Did you have to embarrass the girl like that? We were comparing tattoos. She's just had an amazing one crafted on the back of her hand that goes right up the inside of her forearm. She told me it took over eight hours to design."

Sam rolled her eyes and raised a hand to stop him. "I don't want to know. You know how I feel about those damn things." She sat and glanced at his empty plate.

"Sorry, but I think they're cool. Not everyone is a stick-in-the-mud like you. I find it interesting to understand people's perceptions when they have certain tattoos. I've never seen one like hers before..."

"Bob, enough! No offence, but you'll have to forgive me. I'm just not interested. If you must know, they turn my stomach."

"You can be such a misery guts, stuck in your ways. No, make that a dinosaur..."

"Thanks for the insult. Can we get back on topic and discuss the investigation now?"

"I rest my case," he mumbled.

"Sorry, but I'd rather deal with trying to find a killer in the community than sit here discussing the latest ink someone has decided to deface themselves with. That is the right term, isn't it?"

Bob pushed his plate further away from him. "Actually, there are several names for them these days, like *tight* and *tac*. *Ink*, as you call them, in my opinion, is a bit outdated."

"Each to their own. I dislike them with a passion."

"I think we've established that already."

"Back to the case. Have you spoken to the team?"

"Yes, Claire's arranging everything to be set up here in the morning. Liam and Oliver are on the way over here, now. I assumed you'd want to start canvassing the village right away."

"Yes, we can make a start on that today. You and I will seek out the boyfriend after I've had a cuppa."

"What? It's like something out of a novel," someone shouted behind the counter. "What is it that attracts killers to this village?"

Sam's gaze shifted sideways to see Emma's embarrassed expression. She shrugged at Sam and mouthed an apology before she spoke to Helen, the member of staff who had a notoriously loud voice. Helen turned and waved at Sam. She too mouthed an apology and slapped a hand over her mouth. The other customers hadn't seemed to notice, which was a relief to Sam. For now, the fewer people who knew about the incident, the better.

Emma delivered Sam's coffee personally. "I'm so sorry about Helen. She sometimes forgets how loud she is."

"I'll bear her in mind if I ever leave my bullhorn at home."

The three of them laughed.

"I forgot to ask, Sam. Did you want something to eat?" Emma asked.

"Not for me. I don't think I could stomach anything with what lies ahead of us."

"I'm not surprised. How was your roll, Bob?"

"Great as usual. I'm tempted to have a second one, but I know how Sam would feel about that."

Emma grinned and walked away.

"Don't let me stop you," Sam said. She tore the end of a sugar packet and tipped the contents in her cup. "You've never let me before."

"I'm fine. I was joking. It was a bigger roll than usual, and Helen put some crisps on the side for me."

"Spoiling you, eh?" Sam withdrew her notebook from her pocket and jotted down a few ideas that had been running through her mind.

Bob took a sip from his cup and asked, "What do we know about the boyfriend?"

"Emma told me they were arguing a lot lately."

"Interesting. Are you going to challenge him about that?"

Sam raised an eyebrow. "What do you think?"

Bob tutted and puffed out his cheeks. "All right. Pardon me for stating the obvious. Do we know where he works?"

"No. I'll ask Emma before we leave. She's bound to know. She's a fount of information around here."

"I remember from the last investigation we ran. It's nice being back here but not under these circumstances."

"I agree. It angers me that people come here with the intent to rob someone of their life."

"It's the world we live in. These days, nowhere is truly considered safe. Look how many murders take place either in a church or in a graveyard."

"Wow, that's not something I had considered, but yes, you're right. The world has officially gone nuts."

"You know what they say. More wars have been started over religion than any other topic."

Sam sighed. "That's true." She sipped at her drink and stared out of the window at the hills surrounding them. "Nevertheless, this place exudes tranquillity. Maybe it's just me, but every time I come here, my heart swells with a joy, a feeling I've never encountered before."

"It's your happy place. We're all supposed to have at least one during our lifetime. I've yet to discover mine."

"I suppose. I've never really thought about it that way before. It still shocks me that people can use this place as their wicked playground."

"It shouldn't shock you, I mean, not nowadays." Bob finished the rest of his drink. "I'm ready when you are."

"Give me a chance, it's still boiling hot. I'm trying not to scald my mouth."

2

Twenty minutes later, after Emma had given them the information they needed on where to find Luke, they knocked on his front door. He answered it wearing jogging bottoms and a sweatshirt with the words 'I'm a grumpy human' on the front.

Sam flashed her warrant card. "Hello, Luke. I'm DI Sam Cobbs, and this is my partner, DS Bob Jones. Would it be all right if we came in and spoke with you for a moment?"

He frowned and glanced over Sam's shoulder at Bob. "The police? Have I done something wrong?"

"No. We'd like to speak with you as part of our enquiries, sir."

His frown deepened. "What enquiries?"

"It would be better if we came in."

He stood back and gestured for them to enter the snug hallway. "You'd better come through to the lounge, the first door on the right behind you."

"Is it all right if we keep our shoes on?"

"Of course. It's dry outside, for now. That's due to change later, so the weatherman told us earlier."

The three of them took a seat in the lounge. Luke sat on the edge of his armchair while Sam and Bob sat on the leather sofa.

"Perhaps you can tell me what this visit is about?"

"It's with regret that we're here to tell you that your girlfriend, Angel Pritchard, was found dead up at the lake this morning."

His head jutted forward, and he reached for his phone. He scrolled through it and rang a number. "No, this can't be true. I'm going to call her now."

Sam shook her head. "She won't answer. I'm so sorry for your loss. We've already broken the sad news to her mother."

"Oh God, I can't believe what I'm hearing. Up the lake? How did she die? She loved it up there and went for a hike whenever she could when she wasn't teaching."

"We won't know the actual cause of death until the pathologist gives us his report."

"Pathologist? Is she up there now? Can I see her? Or is that a stupid question? What state is her body in? Shit, I can't believe I asked that. I didn't mean it that way. The right words aren't coming out. I'm sorry. What I meant to ask was if her body is damaged. Shit, that came out wrong again. If I went up there, would I be able to recognise her?"

"I want to assure you that she's being taken care of by the pathologist and his team. There would be no point in you going up there. You wouldn't be allowed near her body."

His head dipped, and his hands covered his face. His shoulders jiggled as he cried.

Sam looked over at Bob and shook her head. His mouth turned down at the sides. It was obvious that her partner was feeling the emotion, too.

"Can we get you a drink, Luke?"

He released his hands and stared at her. "Yes, I could do with a brandy. There's a bottle on the side in the kitchen."

"Bob, would you mind getting Luke a drink, please?"

"The glasses are in the cupboard above," Luke called after him when Bob left the room. "I'm sorry for breaking down like that. Before she left this morning, we had an argument."

Sam withdrew her notebook from her pocket and flipped it open. "May I ask what it was about?"

"We haven't been seeing eye to eye on a lot of things lately. Actually, it was more than that. Angel told me a few weeks ago that she wanted to end our relationship."

"Oh, I see. How long have you been together?"

"Just over a year, I think. My work is full-on most days. I work really long hours. She accused me of neglecting her. The thing is, she ran a few classes in the evening, which meant that we couldn't spend as much time together as we did in the beginning, when we first started seeing each other."

"Whose house is this?"

"It's hers. She invited me to move in three weeks after we started dating. Around that time, I applied for a promotion at work, not thinking I would get it. Unfortunately, I did. That's where all our problems started. I was eager to show my boss that he'd chosen the right man for the job. To do so, I had to work extra hours, which caused friction between Angel and me. She stood it for so long and then told me we'd drifted too far apart. She couldn't take it any more and told me to move out."

Sam glanced up from the notes she was taking and asked, "I understand. So why are you still here?"

"Because I can't find a suitable place to live. Maybe I'm being too fussy. The trouble is, my job doesn't give me the time to go flat- or house-hunting."

"And what did Angel think about that?"

"She told me not to rush, to ensure the move was right. I gave her the space she needed. I'm now in the spare room. We got on great as friends."

"If that's the case, why did you tell me earlier that you'd argued with her this morning?"

His gaze dropped to the carpet in front of him. "Because she told me someone had shown interest in her and that she wanted to start dating again."

"But if you'd broken up, why would her personal life matter to you?"

Bob entered the room and handed the glass of brandy to Luke.

He took a large gulp and then stared at the amber liquid. "How would you feel? I couldn't bear the thought of her moving on, not while I was still living in the house."

"What was she supposed to do? Put her life on hold until you'd got yourself sorted out?"

"No, I didn't want that. If you must know, I thought there was a chance we'd get back together."

"Ah, okay, well, that's a different story then. Have you been here all morning?"

"Yes. I had a few conference calls to make, one with my boss and two others with members of my team. I can show you the calls I've made today on my computer, if it will help."

"Thanks, there's no rush. We just need to verify that you were here all morning."

"I was. I know I'm bound to be a suspect, what with recently breaking up with her, but I can assure you, I wouldn't lay a finger on her. I still loved her and was trying to entice her back."

"I'm sorry. I know this has probably come as a shock to you. Can you tell me if she's had any issues with anyone recently?"

"Issues?"

"Any disagreements with anyone other than yourself?"

"I wouldn't know. She stopped confiding in me long ago."

"That's a shame. What about this other fella who was interested in her? Can you tell me more about him?"

"I can't. She didn't tell me what his name was, only that she'd met him at the local book club."

Sam wrote down the information. Maybe Emma would know more about him. "Okay, what about the neighbours? Everything hunky-dory with them?"

"Yes, we get on great with everyone around here. They're going to be devastated to hear the news. I'm sorry I can't give you any further information. I know how difficult it is to begin your investigation when the clues and evidence are thin on the ground."

Sam tilted her head. "Tell me more."

"Sorry, I should have told you. My father is a retired police officer."

"Did he serve in this area?"

"Yes, for a couple of years. He served most of his time in Norfolk, where we used to live. That's another reason why I can't be responsible for her death. Dad would skin me alive if I ever stepped out of line."

Sam smiled and nodded. "As most fathers would, even more so if they used to be in the Force. What's his name?"

"Ian Walcott. Do you know him?"

"Yes, I vaguely remember the name. Right, if there's nothing else you can tell us, then I think we're done here."

"I'm sorry, I haven't been much use to you. I feel guilty for not being able to tell you more."

"Don't worry."

"What about Maria? How did she take the news?"

"As expected, I suppose. She was distraught. You might want to show your support, possibly go round to see her, that is, if you're still on speaking terms."

"We are. I'll go round there right away, sod my job for a change. Maybe if I hadn't been distracted by my work, Angel would still be with us today."

"There's no way of knowing if that could be true or not."

He rose to his feet and then frowned. "Wait, I've just thought about something."

"What's that?" Sam asked, also getting to her feet.

"Why are you asking if she'd fallen out with anyone? You wouldn't be asking such questions if she had died from natural causes, would you?"

Sam nodded. "You're right. I'm just covering all the bases. As I've already told you, the cause of death won't come to light until the post-mortem has been carried out."

"But you believe there are suspicious circumstances surrounding her death, don't you? Please be honest with me."

"Possibly. That's as much as I can tell you right now."

He showed them to the door.

Sam shook his hand. "Thanks for answering our questions."

"Wait, you need to see proof that I attended the calls this morning, don't you?"

"Ah, yes. If you wouldn't mind."

"My office is in the dining room. It's this way."

He led them into the room next door and wiggled his mouse to bring his computer screen to life. "Here's a list of all the calls I made this morning."

On the list were several calls made between ten and twelve, all of varying lengths, but Sam could see there was no break between them, only a matter of seconds. "That's great. Thanks for showing us."

She and Bob left the house and went back to the car. "What's your take on him?" Sam asked.

"He seemed a nice enough chap. It's clear that he still loves her. Or should I say loved her? What about you? Anything prodding that gut feeling of yours?"

"Plenty. Oh, I don't know. Maybe he was jealous of the attention this other man was showing her and decided to take it out on her instead of him."

"Possibly. Although I doubt it. What about the calls he made? He wouldn't have had the chance to get up to the lake, find her location and get back here. Or am I missing something?"

"No, I think you're right. Let's keep him in mind going forward. I think we'd be foolish not to. I'm going to nip back to The Gather and ask if Emma knows who this other fella was." Sam drove the five hundred yards back to the café, her head whirling with different scenarios, none of them making any sense this early in the investigation. "Do you want to stay here? I won't be long."

With that, Liam and Oliver arrived and parked up beside them.

"I'll bring the others up to date on things."

"Good idea."

Sam waved at the boys and dashed back into the café. Emma was passing the front door on her way into the office with a sneaky bacon roll in her hand.

"Naughty."

"I know. I'm supposed to be on a diet. Hey-ho. Did you forget something?"

"No. I wanted to ask you a few questions, if that's all right."

"Come through to the office. I can eat and talk at the same time."

They both sat.

"I've just visited Luke. He told me that a bloke at the book club had asked Angel out. Did you know anything about that?"

"Oh, gosh, what will you think of me keeping that information from you? In truth, I didn't know Nathan had asked her out. Angel told me they had started attending the book club together, but I didn't know things had escalated."

"Nathan? Do you know his surname?"

"Let me think." She took a bite from her roll. The aroma made Sam's stomach rumble. "Do you want me to get you one?"

"No, I'm fine. You're not the only one who has to watch what she eats."

"Like hell, there's nothing to you."

"Since being with Rhys, I've put on a few extra pounds. He's such a wonderful cook; I can't say no to the meals he puts in front of me. I was brought up not to leave anything on my plate."

"Yep, that's my trouble as well. Nathan Stevens. He's a local in the village, although he works in Workington during the day. He makes windows at the factory out there."

"Do you know which one?"

Emma shook her head. "Sorry, I don't know. He lives in one of the cottages in the village, down by the river, if that helps."

"I think I know the ones you mean. Asking the obvious here, do you know what time he finishes?"

"I should imagine around five. That would be a guess on my part, sorry."

"No problem. Okay, I'll leave you to enjoy your lunch. Thanks again, Emma. We'll be back in the morning, if that's all right with you?"

"It is." She pushed her roll away from her. "I've gone off it now."

"Sorry, that's my fault, reminding you why we're here."

"Not at all. Don't worry about it. Good luck with the investigation. You know where I am if you need any gossip about the villagers."

"I do. Thanks again."

Sam left the café and jumped back into the car. Liam and Oliver were sitting in the back.

"If you guys haven't had lunch yet, I suggest you grab something before we start canvassing the area."

"We had a sandwich back at the station," Liam replied.

"Right, Emma has given me the name of the man who was interested in Angel. Nathan Stevens. He's a window manufacturer at a factory in Workington. Anyone know offhand how many window companies there are in Workington?"

"Off the top of my head I can think of two situated on the outlying trading estates," Oliver said.

Bob tapped the information into his phone. "I've got a dodgy reception at present; it might take a few minutes until I can give you a more accurate answer."

Not what Sam needed to hear. "It is what it is out here, something we're going to need to be mindful about during the investigation. Oliver, can you think of the names?"

"I'm trying. Let me check." Oliver received a better reception due to having a different provider than Bob, and he came back with the answer within seconds. "Lakeside Windows and Morton Windows. The second one is a family-run business."

"Brilliant. Can you give both of them a call and see which one Nathan works for, please?"

Oliver was already dialling the first number by the time Sam was halfway through her request. "Hi, I'm DC Oliver Lucas, calling from

Cumbria Constabulary. I wonder if you could tell me if you have a Nathan Stevens working for you?" He put the phone on speaker so everyone could hear the reply.

"Yes, we do. Did you want to speak with him?"

Oliver covered the mouthpiece. "Do you, boss?"

"Not yet. Just thank her and we'll catch up with him later. No, wait, ask the woman what time he's due to finish."

"Hi, I'm back. Sorry about that. Umm... not just now. Can you tell me what time he finishes work?"

"We shut down the machines at five. The workforce is usually off the premises by five-fifteen at the latest. Do you want me to tell him you'd like to speak to him?"

"No, it's fine. We'll catch up with him another time. One last question, if I may. Has he been there all day?"

"As far as I know. I could check with his line manager if you want me to," the helpful secretary responded.

"No, don't bother. Thanks for your help." Oliver ended the call.

"That solves that particular query, for now," Sam said. "I suggest we start canvassing Angel's closest neighbours next. I need you to ask the usual questions: what time did she leave the house? Has anyone noticed Walcott leave the residence today? I know we've seen evidence of the calls he's made today, but there's no harm in double-checking. Also, we need to find out if anyone strange has been hanging around the village or outside Angel's house within the last week or so. That's it, guys. Follow me, I'll take you to where Angel and Walcott live."

Liam and Oliver left the car. Sam reversed out of her spot in the tight car park and took a left at the bottom onto the main road that led back to the village. Once they were over the bridge, she indicated right and pulled into a gap large enough for Oliver to park directly behind her.

The team split up and canvassed the neighbours. About an hour later, they met up at the end of the street and compared notes. Disappointingly, the results were all the same: a big fat zero.

"I hate it when that happens, and frankly, it's all too often lately."

"Maybe it shows how disinterested people are these days," Bob suggested.

"Ordinarily, I'd agree with you, but in the past, this village, or should I say its residents, have always proved to be observant and eager to help us."

"Yeah, that's true. Where do we go from here, then?" Bob asked. He nudged Sam's arm and nodded towards the pathologist's van as it approached.

Sam waved Des down and stepped forward to speak to him. "How did it go up there? Anything else of interest show up after we left?"

"Nothing. We did what we had to do on site. I was eager to get on the road before the rain started. We encountered a brief hailstorm up there as it was. Luckily, by then, we had loaded the victim in the back of the van. How's it going with you?"

"It's not. Not really. We've discovered that Angel lived with her former boyfriend. They split up weeks ago, although he still lives at the property. His alibi checks out, and none of the neighbours saw him leave the property today. We've also discovered that Angel was keen to start dating someone else. He lives in the village and works in Workington. We're hoping to catch up with him later."

Des gestured for her to get on with it.

"You can be a pain in the arse at times. I'm going as fast as I can. I've also informed the victim's mother. Sadly, she lost her husband last year and was distraught to learn that Angel had also lost her life."

"I'm not surprised. Poor woman. Does she want to see the body?"

"I didn't ask. She was desperate to get home. I caught up with her up at the café; the manager introduced us. That's about it, for now."

"Good. I'm going to crack on with the PM as soon as I get back. Hopefully, I'll let you know my findings by the end of the day."

"That would be superb, if it happens. I hope all goes well. Are SOCO hanging around up there?"

"They are. They should be finished soon." He mock-saluted, revved his engine and drove off.

"He's got that down to a fine art," Bob said as she rejoined the others.

"What's that?"

"Winding you up."

Sam growled and walked back to the car to mull over which part of the village they should canvass next. Time was marching on. The kids were emerging with their parents from the primary school at the end of the road. She pondered whether they should go back to The Gather before she realised it would probably be shut by now. That notion was confirmed a few minutes later when she saw Grace and another member of staff cross the road outside the school.

She brought up the map of the village on her phone and pointed to a few of the outlying houses that she wanted Liam and Oliver to cover while she and Bob canvassed the properties close to where she suspected Nathan lived. That way, she could keep an eye open for when the man himself came home. The residents seemed friendly enough, although a couple of them appeared either suspicious or upset as soon as they opened the door to Sam. However, the response to all of her questions was negative. One woman, a young mother called Zoe, who turned out to be Angel's friend, was beside herself when Sam shared the news of Angel's death.

"Oh shit. I was up there with her this morning. We set off together. I had to come back not long after we started because my little one was sick. I thought it would be best to come home because the weather seemed to be changing for the worse up there. Angel is a seasoned walker; she doesn't care what the weather is like as long as she gets her steps in every day. Shit, shit, shit, poor Maria, she's going to be traumatised by this news."

Sam nodded. "I've already told her. Can you remember what time you left Angel and where? It might help us pinpoint the time of her death."

"Bear in mind, I have an active two-year-old, and most of the time I have no idea what time it is. I know we went in my car and, as far as I can remember, I picked her up at around nine thirty and think I was back home by ten at the latest. No, I'm pretty certain now, it was around ten. We left her before the second bridge up there, the one they've recently replaced."

"On the left? Would that be the one which joins the track that leads you back up to the main road?"

"That's the one. I felt bad about leaving her. She was intending to make her own way home. She's nuts like that, a total exercise freak. Or she was. Oh, heck, I need to sit down. My legs are wobbling."

"It's the shock setting in. Can I come in?"

"Yes, of course."

Sam entered the house and closed the door behind her. Zoe took her into the small kitchen at the rear of the terraced house, pulled out a chair at the kitchen table then reached down and picked up her daughter.

"What's her name?"

"Fay. She was named after my grandma. The old-fashioned names are coming back into fashion now, apparently."

"I like it. How is she now?"

"She seems okay. I'm keeping an eye on her. My other daughter is back at school. She's been off with a sickness bug, probably passed it on to you, hasn't she, sweetheart?" Zoe kissed her daughter's cheek. The child squirmed in her lap, desperate to get back on the play mat with her toys. "Go play, cherub, while Mummy talks to her new friend."

"Are we all right talking in front of her?" Sam asked cautiously.

"Yes, once she starts playing with her dolls, she gets lost in a world of her own." That being said, Zoe still lowered her voice to ask, "How did Angel die?"

"The honest answer is, we're not sure yet."

Puzzled, Zoe asked, "I don't understand. Did she fall? Have a heart attack? Slip and lose her footing and tumble into the lake? You must be able to give me some sort of answer."

Sam looked her in the eye and answered truthfully, "At first glance, we believe she may have fallen. Unfortunately, we won't be able to give a definitive answer until the pathologist gives us his report."

"Oh my, the thought of her... no, I can't say it. One of my favourite

TV programmes is *Silent Witness*; however, the thought of her... you know."

"I understand what you're getting at. The pathologist will take care of her. It's important that a post-mortem is carried out. It's the only way for us to establish what caused her death."

Zoe ran a hand over her face, then through her hair, and glanced down at her daughter playing happily beside her. "I'm struggling to take it in. I have so many questions in my head that I know you won't be able to answer, given what you've already told me. Damn, why did I leave her up there alone? I should have stayed with her. Maybe if I had... she would still be alive."

Sam reached across the table and rested her hand on Zoe's forearm. "I'm sorry. You had a sick child. She was your priority at the time. You can't have any remorse about the situation."

"About fate, you mean?"

"That's right. I truly believe our lives are mapped out for us; they have to be, don't they? Otherwise, everyone would live until they're in their eighties or nineties, wouldn't they?"

"I suppose you're right. I've never really had cause to think about it before. I'll miss her so much. We've been friends since primary school. She was one of my bridesmaids when Warren and I got married. Gosh, that seems a lifetime ago." Tears formed in her eyes, despite her trying to hold it together in front of her daughter.

"Why don't I give your husband a call and ask him to come home and be with you?"

"No, you can't. He's away for the day on a business trip. It was an overnight one; he's due back around six. He'll be on his way home now, anyway."

"I'm glad you won't be alone. Are you all right to answer a few more questions? Not many, I promise."

"Yes, I think so. I want to do all I can to help you."

"During your recent conversations with Angel, has she mentioned that she'd fallen out with anyone or had any sort of problem with either someone she knew or had recently met?"

Zoe stared at her daughter as she thought. "No... erm, sorry that's not quite true. I assume, you're aware of her living with Luke Walcott?"

"Yes, I called round to see him earlier. He was honest about their breakup. Actually, he was the one who told us about Nathan. I didn't sense there was any animosity there. He said he was trying to find another place to live, but it was proving difficult for him."

"Again, that proves what a gem Angel was. When they broke up, she didn't have it in her to tell him to pack his bags. I would have if he were my ex. The arguments had escalated into a daily occurrence. I was the one who urged her to give him the boot because I felt he was taking advantage of her good nature. She'd already confided in me that her feelings towards him had altered. She was young enough to find someone more suitable. I also encouraged her to get out more, to join a few clubs and meet people. That's when she heard about the book club they hold at The Gather and how she met Nathan."

"She didn't know him before, despite living in the same village?"

"She knew of him but had never really held a conversation with him. Neither had I, come to that. Just because you live in a small community like this, it doesn't mean you know everyone."

Sam shrugged. "I suppose you're right. I live in a small village on the outskirts of Workington, so I know better than most how true that statement is."

"I really hoped their friendship would develop into a relationship, but there was little hope of that happening while she allowed Luke to live under the same roof. But she was coming around to the idea of asking him to get his finger out and find other accommodation. No chance of him doing that now, is there? What would be the point?"

"He'll still need to find somewhere else to live. He told me himself that the house belonged to Angel."

"Well, Angel and the bank," Zoe corrected.

Fay suddenly started screaming. The ear-piercing noise cut through Sam like a knife.

"I'm sorry, she's hurt herself." She swooped down and picked up her daughter. "Hush, now. Mummy will kiss it better."

"There's no need to apologise. You see to her. I think we've covered everything we need to. I'll show myself out. Thank you for talking to me. Take care."

"Thanks. When will we know the outcome of the PM?"

"Should be within a few days. Maybe Maria will tell you if you're friendly with her."

"I'll call round there and see her tomorrow to make sure she's okay. My other daughter should be home soon. My mum picked her up from school for me while I dealt with Fay. I can give them the all-clear to come home now. She doesn't seem too bad now. A bit niggly, but that's normal at that age."

"I wouldn't know. I don't have children."

Zoe saw Sam to the front door. "Through choice? Because you're a police officer and career-driven?"

"Yes, through choice." She didn't have the heart to tell her that she had discussed having IVF with Chris, her former husband, before they'd split up. "I think I'm too old now."

"Get away with you. You must be only about thirty-three or thirty-four, aren't you?"

"I'll soon be thirty-five. I'm not sure I'd have the patience to take on another human being at my age." She laughed and left the house, ensuring the conversation ended there. It was a subject that she and Rhys hadn't discussed, so she had no idea if he wanted children in the future or not. Maybe they should do that before they thought about setting a date for their wedding. "Thanks for chatting with me. Sorry it was under such sad circumstances. Take care of yourself."

"Thank you. Good luck with your investigation."

Sam crossed the road to wait for Bob, who was speaking to an older man on his doorstep. While she waited, she glanced up and down the road. That's when she spotted a white van pull up outside one of the terraced cottages close to the river.

She sprinted down the road and called out, "Hello, are you Nathan Stevens?"

The man, who was in his late twenties, faced her. "That's right. Who wants to know?"

Sam felt Bob sneak up behind her, doing his best to catch up with her.

"I'm DI Sam Cobbs of the Cumbria Constabulary. I'd like to have a chat with you if it's convenient."

"Ah, right. The secretary at work told me an officer had called the factory, enquiring about me. I was puzzled to hear that. What's this about?"

Sam caught up with him, her breathing laboured but not as heavy as Bob's when he stopped beside her. "This is my partner, DS Bob Jones. You haven't done anything wrong; we're making general enquiries about an incident that happened this morning. Can we come in for a chat?"

"Yes, I have nothing to hide. What type of incident? And, by the way, I've been at work all day. My line manager can vouch for me on that front."

"We're aware. The secretary corroborated that fact when I called earlier."

He opened the door to his home and removed his shoes. Sam and Bob followed suit by taking theirs off.

"Come in. Do you want a drink? I'm going to make myself a coffee if that's all right with you."

"A coffee would be most welcome, thanks," Sam replied. "White with one sugar for both of us. Have you lived here long?"

"In the village or in this house?"

"Both," Sam replied as they relocated to the larger-than-average kitchen at the rear of the property.

"Take a seat. I've lived in the village all my life but only gathered enough funds to put down a deposit on this place two years ago. It's mortgaged to the hilt, so I'm not sure if I can call it mine." He laughed.

"I know that feeling," Sam agreed. "It's in a lovely setting, right by the river."

"Yes, I'd often walked past this place and thought about owning it, as you do. The old owner died. It needed a total renovation before I could move in. My two brothers and my parents helped me whip it into shape. I'm lucky in that respect. One of my brothers is a builder and the other is a plumber, so we had all the trades covered, what with me working at the window factory. I persuaded my boss to give me a good deal on the windows. As a family, we were down here every night, give or take, and every weekend. Hard work turned this place around in eight weeks. We're all really pleased with the result."

"Wow, that's a seriously impressive accomplishment. I'm not surprised you and your family are proud of your achievement."

"We are. I'll be in debt to them for the rest of my life, but it was worth it."

"It's great to have a family supportive enough to see a job through until the end."

He poured the boiling water into the mugs he had prepared and delivered the drinks to the table and benches, which appeared to be made from scaffold planks.

Sam ran her hand over the table. "Are these what I think they are?"

"Yes, my friend is a carpenter. He got his hands on a job lot of scaffold planks and decided to make some bespoke furniture. All my friends admired the set. He's been inundated with orders and has had to set up a sideline, which he works on in his spare time at the weekend."

"I'd love his name and address if you have it. I've been renovating my cottage, and I think something like this is just what I've been looking for to enhance my kitchen."

He crossed the room to the dresser along the far wall and returned with a card. "Here, have this one. I know where to find him."

Sam smiled. "I appreciate it. Thanks very much."

Nathan sat on the bench opposite them and interlocked his fingers around his mug. "Right, why don't you tell me why you're here?"

Sam swallowed down the acid burning her throat. "Unfortunately, I have some bad news for you."

His brow furrowed into deep creases. "And that is?"

"We were called out to an incident this morning up at the lake. A body had been found up there."

He shifted slightly in his seat, as if knowing what Sam was about to say next.

"Unfortunately, it was Angel Pritchard."

He started shaking his head as soon as Sam mentioned the victim's first name. "No, this can't be true. Are you sure it was her? She's so athletic and she knows the route up there so well. How did she die?" His gaze dropped to his mug.

"We're not sure what the cause of death is yet. We've been told that you were interested in asking her out. Is that true?"

His head shot up, and he stared at Sam. "What are you saying? That I had something to do with her death? Was she murdered? Is that what you're telling me?"

"Please, I wasn't suggesting anything of the sort. All we're trying to figure out is if someone had any intention of deliberately going after her. Did she mention to you if she was worried about anyone?"

"No. And for your information, we had our first date during the week. We arranged to meet up at the book club. After that, we went to the Fox and Hounds, and time flew past. We ended up getting kicked out of there at closing time. I walked Angel home, well, part of the way. She told me to leave her at the bottom of her road in case Luke saw us together."

"He wasn't aware that you'd started dating?"

"No, she was plucking up the courage to tell him. She'd hinted that I had asked her out, just to see what his reaction was."

"And how was it?" Sam probed.

"He went for her—verbally, I'm talking about, not physically. If he'd laid a hand on her, I would have gone round there and wiped the floor with him. She was desperate to get him out of the house. It was getting to the point where it was playing on her mind all the time. I know Zoe, her best friend, was pushing for her to see sense and to kick him out. The trouble with Angel was that she had a good heart, which proved to be detrimental when she needed to be more forceful with him. I told her I would have a word with Luke, but she pleaded with me not to get involved. She told me she was getting braver, dropping huge hints for him to get his arse into gear, as it were. Hang on, you don't think he's behind this, do you?"

Sam raised a hand. "No, I don't believe so. We visited him earlier, and he gave us proof of where he was at the time of her death."

"Doesn't mean he wasn't involved. He could have paid someone to kill her, or perhaps I'm thinking too far out of the box?"

"I have to tell you, from what we've learnt, we haven't dismissed him out of hand. What about anyone else in the village or the surrounding area? Can you think of anyone else she's had an issue with recently?"

"No. I know we'd only just started seeing each other, but I've known of her for a while. I can't say I've ever heard anyone speak badly about her, not around here."

"Thank you, that's the sort of information we need to hear. Zoe said pretty much the same. Which would lead us to believe that either Angel had an accident, or she was in the wrong place at the wrong time when someone attacked her. Again, we won't know if it's the latter until after we've received the pathologist's report."

"If there's anything I can do to help, you only have to ask. If she was targeted by someone, everyone in this village would be shocked to learn that information."

"The more canvassing we do in the area in the meantime, the more likely we are to discover if anyone had a grudge against her. From what we've learnt so far, nothing could be further from the truth. Okay, we'll leave things there for now. Here's one of my cards. If you should either hear or think of anything that we should know about..."

"I'll ring you straight away."

After drinking their coffee, they returned to the front door. Sam and Bob put their shoes on and shook his hand before they left the property.

Outside, they found Liam and Oliver walking down the hill towards the river.

"Any luck?" Sam asked, not expecting them to have had any success, either.

"Nothing, boss. Very disappointing. Apparently, Angel was a popular figure in the village."

"Yes, that's the impression I'm getting as well. No one has told us that she'd fallen out with anyone, well, except for Luke, her ex-boyfriend." She waved her level hand from side to side. "I'm still on the fence about him. I'll ask Claire to do the necessary digging on him in the morning, just in case. Let's call it a day and start over again first thing."

The rest of the team seemed as downhearted as she was to be calling it a day without obtaining any useful information that might get the investigation started. The joys of being a police officer!

SAM DROVE HOME, eager to see Rhys. She had it in mind to change her shoes as soon as she got in and take Casper and Sonny for a long walk to help clear her mind. However, Rhys' car wasn't there when she got home. She instantly went into panic mode after what had happened to him a few months back.

Doreen, her neighbour, was standing at her lounge window, smiling and waving at her. Beside her was the love of both their lives, Sonny, Sam's cockapoo, whom Doreen had volunteered to look after during the day since he was a pup.

Sam locked the car and rang Rhys' number. The voicemail kicked in, causing her more concern. She left him a message. "I'm home. Any idea how long you're going to be?" She kept her tone and conversation light, not wanting to let on how worried she was.

Doreen opened the door to greet her. "Everything all right, love? You seem worried."

"Just concerned because Rhys isn't home yet."

"Ah, I see. I'm sure he won't be long. Do you want to come in for a cuppa?"

Sam smiled, grateful for her neighbour's thoughtfulness. "Why not? I had every intention of taking the dogs for a walk as soon as I got home. I suppose that plan will have to be shelved now." She glanced over her shoulder and up the road before she closed the door behind her.

"What sort of day have you had?"

"A frustrating one. A new case came our way this morning up at Ennerdale, and we're still waiting for the first clue to jump out at us. Well, apart from an ex-boyfriend who could be our one and only suspect." Sam joined Doreen in her old-fashioned kitchen. Sonny bounced around beside her, happy that she was finally home, which meant a long walk was on the cards.

"But you're not sure it's the ex. Is that what you're saying?"

"Yes, I have grave doubts. He's given us an alibi which puts him in the clear. We'll see what the background checks say about him in the morning. Enough about me. How are you doing? You appear to be moving easier now you're recovering from your surgery, are you?"

"Yes, I no longer have pain in my hips; well, maybe a small niggle now and then. It's lovely to be able to throw the ball for Sonny when he brings it to me in the garden. He's a treasure. I absolutely adore him. I thought he might change a little, you know, what with Casper moving in and him not being the centre of attention all the time."

"I think he surprised us all in that respect." She ruffled his head and bent to kiss him on the nose. "He's adorable, and you know it, don't you, Munchkin?"

He bounced beside her again. Sam removed her phone from her pocket to see if she'd missed a message from Rhys. She hadn't.

"Hey, I'm sure he's fine and you're worrying about nothing," Doreen said. She handed Sam a mug of coffee. "He'll be home by the time you've drunk that, guaranteed. Do you want to sit in the garden?"

The evenings were getting longer and warmer, and so they should be. They were approaching June now. After last year's dire summer and the longest winter Sam could ever remember enduring, they were all ready for a change in the weather. In her experience, having the sun out every day put people in a different mood.

No sooner had they sat down than the doorbell rang. Sam jumped out of her seat to answer it. "I'll get it. It's bound to be Rhys."

She opened the door to see him standing there, and her heart skipped several beats. "Thank God. Where have you been? I tried calling you."

He winced and whispered, "Sorry" against her lips. Pulling back from their kiss, he checked his mobile. "Damn, I forgot to take it off silent. I had a late client and packed up to come home the second he left."

"It doesn't matter, well, it does, but you're home now. Where's Casper?"

"I let him in the house. Should I get him?"

"Why not? I'm having a cuppa with Doreen in the back garden. Do you want one?"

"No, not for me. I think the boys could do with a walk. Why don't I take them while you have a natter with Doreen?"

"No, I want to come. Let me spend five minutes with her and then we'll shoot off."

He slipped into the house and collected Casper. She left the door open, and Casper came bounding through Doreen's kitchen and into the garden. The dogs leapt around with joy at the sight of each other. Sam threw the ball for them, and they both took off, eager to get it first.

"How was your day?" she asked Rhys.

"Hit and miss. What about you?"

"Pretty much the same. I'll tell you about it later. Doreen was just telling me how good her hip is now."

"That's excellent news, Doreen. I saw you hanging out the washing the other day. I was spying on you from the back bedroom window. You appeared to be taking everything in your stride. I didn't notice you were in any pain. We've been worried about you."

"You're too sweet. There's no need to worry about me. Should I be alarmed that you're spying on me?"

They all laughed.

"I knew as soon as I said it that it could be misinterpreted," Rhys said, his cheeks colouring up.

Sam tapped him on the knee. "That'll teach you to be a peeping Tom."

"I need to monitor what I say in the future. That's for sure."

The dogs came bounding towards him, and once Casper had surrendered the ball, he threw it again.

"They're bundles of energy. I sometimes think they lead the best lives out of all of us," Doreen said.

"It is wonderful to see them having so much fun." Sam downed the rest of her drink and stood. "And on that note, they clearly need their trip to the park. That is, if you don't mind us running out on you like this, Doreen?"

"You do what you have to do. I only wish I was fit enough to come with you."

"It's a shame. Maybe we can take a ride to the beach at the weekend. You could come with us. We'd have to take two cars, but that shouldn't be a problem."

"That would be lovely. Thank you for thinking about me, Sam."

"Always." Sam pecked her on the cheek and took her empty mug into the kitchen. "Are you and the boys ready?" she called out to Rhys.

"We are. Casper, Sonny, do you want to go for a walk?"

THEY RETURNED from their walk nearly an hour later.

"I think we all needed an extra stroll today. What's on the menu for this evening?" Sam asked.

"How about homemade fish and chips?" Rhys said. "Umm... that might have been a tad misleading. What I should have suggested was, how about frozen fish and chips, as opposed to nipping out to the chippy?"

Sam chuckled. "Either sounds good to me. Do you need a hand?"

"Nope. Can you sort out the dogs and feed and water them for me?"

"My pleasure." Sam removed the food they had prepared at the weekend for them and filled both bowls, then topped up their larger water bowl. Both dogs wolfed down the contents in no time at all. "Two satisfied customers. Glad I don't eat that quickly—I'd get indigestion." Sam's mobile vibrated across the worktop. She picked it up to see Des's name on the screen. "Sorry, I need to take this."

"It's fine. You worry too much."

She smiled and turned her back on him. "Hi, Des. How's it going?"

"Sorry to disturb you so late, Sam. I thought you'd want to know the results of Angel Pritchard's PM straight away."

"You thought right. What was the cause of death?"

"Bruising came out on her face during the examination."

"Meaning she was hit?" Sam sat at the table and stared at the wall.

"No. She had bruising around her mouth as though someone was eager to hold her in position. I ran some initial toxicology tests. We'll have to wait for the proper information to come back, but my early assessment would be that Angel was forced to ingest something that ultimately led to her death."

"What the…? Are we talking about some form of poison?"

"Possibly, yes. I just thought you should know ASAP."

"I appreciate it, thanks, Des. Well, this sheds a different light on the investigation."

"It does. How did you get on today?"

"We had a very frustrating day. The only suspect on our radar is the ex-boyfriend who was still living with her. Unfortunately, he has a pretty solid alibi. We'll be carrying out the background checks on him in the morning."

"Well, good luck with that. I'll push the results through for you. That way you'll know what substances were used to poison her."

"Great news. Thanks, Des. Enjoy the rest of your evening."

"Not going to happen. I've been informed there's been a crash with fatalities just north of Workington."

"Ouch! That sounds awful. I'll wait to hear from you."

"Should be within a day or two. It was definitely murder, staged to convince us that she'd fallen from the ledge, which we were both dubious about at the time."

"Ain't that the truth? I hope you don't have to work too late. Thanks for getting in touch."

"Me too."

He ended the call. Sam's mind whirled with the information he'd given her.

Rhys squeezed her shoulder, making her jump. "Sorry, I didn't mean to startle you. Are you all right?"

"I was in a world of my own. Des reckons the victim was forced to either eat or drink something poisonous."

"Wow, really? Not what you were expecting to hear, was it?"

"No, not in the slightest. Damn. And yet, the feedback we've had from everyone we've spoken to today confirmed that Angel was a kind and decent person. So why the heck would someone set out to kill her?"

"Could it be that she was in the wrong place at the wrong time?" Rhys opened the air fryer drawer and turned the contents.

"In truth, I don't know what to believe. Not tonight, not without doing further digging. How long before dinner? Do I have time to change?"

"Yes, another ten minutes. What do you want, peas or beans?"

"I fancy beans for a change."

"Beans it is then."

She made her way out of the kitchen. He called out her name, and she poked her head around the doorframe.

"Yes?"

"Missing you already," he said, and they both laughed.

3

Elliot Carter was enjoying a leisurely stroll around Ennerdale Water. He said hello to everyone he passed; he wasn't one of those grumpy walkers who preferred to ignore people. The sun was shining, and there was no sign of darkness descending yet, so he decided to continue his walk at the top end of the lake. He preferred this location because the walk led through the forest, and there was a very different atmosphere at this end of the lake.

He searched the area, eager to find somewhere he could relieve himself. Checking in both directions to ensure there were no other walkers around, he dived behind the trunk of a large tree. "God, I needed that. I've had one too many cups of coffee at work today." He stepped out to find two figures standing there with their backs to him. "Sorry, needs must. You know what it's like."

The strangers turned to face him. They were wearing masks and gloves. One of them was holding a metal pole by their side.

"What the fuck is going on here? Who are you?" Elliot demanded.

"Your worst nightmare," one of the strangers said.

Before Elliot could either respond or run, the pair pounced on him, whacking him with the pole.

Elliot grunted and dropped to his knees. "Please, don't hurt me.

Do I know you? If it's money you want, you're out of luck. I haven't got any. I'm skint. I'm going through a divorce."

One of the attackers bent down and leaned into his face. "Shut up. I'm sick of hearing your voice already. We know all about you."

He was puzzled by the automated voice and by what the person had said. "What do you mean? Have I upset you in the past? Is that what this is all about?"

"I told you to shut up. Say anything else and I'll break your legs."

The other attacker grabbed his accomplice's arm and pulled them back. They held a whispered conversation, adding to Elliot's perplexity.

One of the strangers withdrew something from the other one's rucksack. Elliot could see it was a roll of tape. The smaller of the two tore a strip off and advanced towards him at speed. They slapped the tape over his mouth. It was then that the penny dropped, and he realised he was in deep trouble. He tried to talk, but the obstruction muffled his words. The hand of fear squeezed his heart. He had trouble fathoming what these individuals wanted from him, except perhaps to punish him for something he might have done in the past.

With his mouth secured, they stood on either side of him, seized an arm each and yanked him to his feet. His head swivelled from side to side, and his eyes widened. He tried to plead for help, but it was pointless. There was no way of making them understand him.

Please, someone help me. Just walk past and chase them off. I've seen so many people out here this evening, and now there's no one around. Why? Please, God, don't let them hurt me...

They relocated to a spot among the trees at the base of one of the hills to their right. He said a silent prayer, the first time he'd actually prayed since he was at school. He was thrown to the ground. He looked up to see the shorter of the two raise the bar above their head and beat him with it. Blow after blow, he tried to scream, but the tape did its job. He heard a couple of his bones break, and the pain was excruciating. Not long after, he passed out, unable to withstand the onslaught.

"We need to deal with him quickly. There were several vehicles in the car park, which means there will still be hikers out here."

"I agree. You've beaten him black and blue. Did you hear his bones crunch?"

"Yep, that was my intention. Even if they find him alive, I wanted him to suffer for the rest of his life."

"He won't survive, not with what we have in store for him."

They both chuckled and then fell silent as voices sounded below them on the path. They crouched and watched the three hikers pass by.

"That was close. We're going to need to keep the noise down and be wary of our surroundings."

"Don't worry and stop treating me like an idiot."

"Sorry, I didn't mean to. Let's get him moved," the shorter one said.

Once the hikers were far enough away from them and had turned the next corner, they picked up Elliot's limp body and moved him thirty feet away. Just by the track, coming out of the field in front of them, was a well. They had discovered it on one of their many hikes.

The shorter one checked Elliot's pulse. "He's still alive. Wait, he's coming around again."

Elliot stared up at them and then quickly scanned his surroundings. He shook his head and tried to talk.

"Shut up, or I'll shut you up."

The bar came crashing down on Elliot's right leg. Again, bones shattered upon impact. The same thing happened when the shorter one struck his left leg.

"That should do. Right, let's get him in the well."

Elliot tried to scream. He squirmed out of their grasps several times.

The taller attacker said, "I'm going to have to knock him out. We won't be able to move him otherwise."

"Do it."

The taller one punched him several times in the face. Elliot's chin dipped onto his chest. He was out cold.

"I'll grab his legs, and you take the weight of his body. Once his legs are in the well, I'll come and help you push him in. Hang on, we need to attach the clue." The shorter one withdrew the handkerchief from the rucksack and tied it through the loop of Elliot's jeans.

Together, they heaved Elliot's body into position. His legs dangled over the side of the well. A stone was dropped into the well, and the water plopped at the bottom.

"Good. There's water in there. Anything to make him less comfortable if he survives the fall."

"*If* being the right word," the taller one said. "Are you sure we're doing the right thing? What if someone finds him and rescues him?"

"They won't. You worry too much. On the count of three, let him go. One... two... three."

They released Elliot's body and watched it strike the sides as it descended the confined space.

After surveying the area and confirming it was clear, they removed their masks and gloves, tucked them into the rucksack and joined the track.

"That was amazing. I get such a thrill from this, don't you?" the shorter one asked.

"Clearly not as much as you. I feel bad about taking someone's life unnecessarily."

"Don't. All this is justified. I'm sick to death of people treating me like I don't exist. They all deserve what's coming to them. If you're having second thoughts, you'd better tell me now."

"No, I suppose I'm okay with it. I can see why you want to punish them. They had no right doing that to you."

"Too right. None of this is done out of spite; I'm not the type. They've upset me and they need to be punished. Two down, a few more to go."

"Aren't you worried about the cops being on site?"

"Not really. Actually, it'll be a blast with them using The Gather. At least, I'll get to hear what's going on first-hand."

"That was a stroke of luck—the officer in charge being friends with Emma."

"Yeah. They used the café for the last investigation that took place in this area. We'll have to be cagey. She's not to be messed with. That partner of hers is a bit dim, though."

"You're awful. He can't be that dumb or he wouldn't have got into the Force in the first place."

"That's true. Maybe he just acts dumb. I'll keep an eye on him."

They walked back to the car in silence, then drove along the narrow, winding lane to the village, where they went their separate ways.

"I'll give you a call later," the shorter one said.

"I'm meeting up with friends. I'll call you when I get back."

"Don't bother if it's going to be late. I've got college in the morning."

"Whatever."

4

Sam paced around the makeshift office upstairs at The Gather while she waited for the rest of the team to arrive. Claire never let her down. She always showed up at least ten minutes before she was due, even out here, away from the station. Bob had called to say he was stuck in traffic just south of Workington. Liam was also there, but they'd had no word from Oliver, as yet.

"Liam, can you ring your partner and see how long he's going to be?"

Liam went into the small hallway to make the call. He reappeared a few seconds later. "He should be here soon. He had to stop off to top up with petrol. He hadn't realised how low he was last night, otherwise he would have done it on the way home."

"That's fine, as long as we know."

Emma had set them up with a flask of coffee to keep them going until the café opened at ten.

"Claire, can you make a start on Luke's background checks? I wasn't going to tell you this until the others got here, but I heard from the pathologist last night. His initial findings indicate that Angel Pritchard ingested some form of poison. She had bruising around her chin, suggesting someone had forced her mouth open."

"My goodness," Claire said, disbelief evident in her tone. "So, we'll be searching for a murder suspect, then?"

"Yes. Des and I both agreed that the way she was found made it look like the fall had been staged. I believe this extra evidence confirms it. Now all we have to find is the killer. Easy, right?"

Claire rolled her eyes. "Needle in a haystack comes to mind. I'll see what I can find about the ex."

"I know he showed us proof of his alibi yesterday, but I have no intention of getting off the fence just yet."

Steps thundered up the stairs, and Oliver appeared in the doorway. "Sorry I'm late, boss."

"You're not. We're still waiting for Bob to get here. Make yourself a drink. I'll hold the meeting when he arrives." She went over what Des had told her.

Oliver poured himself a drink and sat down. "Wowzer. Why would someone do that to her, especially in that location?"

"That's what we've got to find out."

More footsteps sounded, and Bob barged into the room. "Sorry. What have I missed?"

Sam groaned. "Can someone else fill him in? I'm sick of repeating myself."

"Pardon me for breathing. The holdup was unavoidable," he grumbled.

"I know. I apologise." She ended up sharing the news with him, herself.

"Wow. Poison? Do we know what type yet?"

"Still waiting to hear about that. We should get a clearer idea in the next day or two. While you get yourself a drink, I need to get the morning meeting underway."

"Go for it. Expect to hear rumblings. I thought the café would be open and that we'd have bacon rolls to munch on when we got here."

Sam rolled her eyes. "They open at ten, as usual. It'll depend on how far we get whether you get fed or not."

Bob's eyes widened. "Charming. An army can't march on an

empty stomach, just saying." He turned his back on her and poured himself a drink.

Sam ignored the comment and went over everything they had learned so far regarding the key players in the investigation, which in all honesty, didn't truly amount to much. "So, that means we're going to be reliant on what we can find through the social media accounts of Luke, Nathan, and Angel herself. The one thing that is really puzzling me is finding a bookmark at the crime scene."

"Where was it found, boss?"

"I spotted it poking out from under her body. I'm assuming either it fell out of her rucksack during the fall—scratch that, it's still early. It must have been planted there by the murderer. Let's try to find a link on Angel's socials to do with reading." She shook her head again. "Forgive me, lack of sleep last night... Zoe, Angel's best friend, told us that Angel had not long joined a book club that actually meets in this very room. I've been led to believe that Nathan Stevens is also a member of the book club."

"Should we be concerned about his safety? Or do you think he might be the killer?" Claire asked.

"Having spoken to him yesterday, I really didn't get the impression he was nervous talking to me. His demeanour was one of shock when he heard the news. I don't think he was faking his emotions or reactions at all."

"I'll see what I can find out," Claire said. She jotted down some notes on the pad beside her.

"Thanks, Claire. If anyone can find something significant, you can. Let's make a start then, folks."

The team put their heads down, using the computers the tech team had set up for them at short notice that morning. That was why Sam arrived there earlier for her shift and probably why she was still feeling tired. She walked over to the window and gazed out at the amazing view. It made her heart flutter. She had to pull herself away from it a few minutes later.

The team had only just begun their searches but, as Sam drifted around the room, she could see that they were all taking notes, which boded well for an early resolution to the case.

Not long after ten, Emma appeared with a tray of flat white coffees and a selection of bacon and sausage rolls, which piqued Bob's interest. He was all over the feast the second she placed them on the desk beside Sam.

"You're spoiling us. You didn't have to do this, Emma."

"I know. But if it helps capture the killer faster, I'm willing to do just about anything."

Sam shook her head and laughed. "Is that supposed to be logical thinking?"

Emma grinned and shrugged. "I'll leave you to it. I really hadn't intended to disturb you working."

"You haven't. As usual, your timing is impeccable, isn't it, Bob?"

He was standing just behind Sam, already munching on the largest sausage roll on offer. "I should say so. First class as always, Emma. It's much appreciated, especially this morning as I skipped breakfast."

"It's my pleasure. I'll leave you to it."

The team gathered around and each chose a roll that was calling to them. Claire took a bit before she revealed that nothing had shown up in the searches she'd carried out on Luke Walcott.

"I thought as much," Sam replied. "He seemed genuine enough and had no hesitation in showing us the proof that he'd been on several conference calls that morning. I doubt if he would have had the foresight to line them up, although I might be wrong—what with him being an IT specialist," she added, doubting her suggestion as soon as it was out.

"What about Nathan?" Bob asked.

Liam and Oliver both shook their heads.

Liam finished his mouthful first and said, "Nothing untoward showing up. He'd only been friends with Angel for a few months."

"The timeline fits. What sort of thing does he get up to in his spare time? Anything waving a red flag there?"

"Not really. He hikes most of the time. Ventures out with a group of friends. From what I could tell, he's working his way through the Wainwrights."

"He's got more guts than me," Bob chipped in. "Some of those fells are massive. I'd probably get a third of the way up the least challenging one and drop dead."

Sam tutted. "If push came to shove and a loved one's life depended on you getting to them, you'd force yourself to do it."

Bob raised an eyebrow. "You reckon? I'd be the one going into debt, paying someone to rescue the buggers."

"There's no hope for you. Why live up here if you've got no intention of getting out there and setting off on different adventures?"

"That's like asking a Londoner how many times they make the most of going on a cruise down the River Thames."

"All right, point taken. And FYI, I'd much prefer living up here than in the Big Smoke."

Sam strained an ear; it sounded like someone was bounding up the staircase. Emma barged into the room, her face devoid of all colour. Sam rushed over to see what was going on.

"Are you all right, Emma?" Sam latched on to the nearest chair, dragged it towards her and eased her friend into it.

"No. There's someone you should come and see downstairs. Mark Abbots, one of the local farmers... he's umm... discovered a body."

"Shit! Do you want to come with me? You can make the introductions if you're up to it."

Sam helped Emma to her feet, but her legs wobbled and gave way beneath her.

"Can I have a moment?"

"Of course. I know this is the last thing you needed to hear on top of Angel's death. You stay here. Bob and I will have a word with the farmer. Is Helen down there?"

"Yes, she'll point Mark out to you. Sorry, Sam. I'll be okay in a few minutes."

"Come down when you're ready. Bob, let's go. Bring your notebook with you."

They rushed down the stairs and into the café where they found

Helen talking to a man wearing muddy wellies and ripped jeans. She saw Sam enter and gestured for her to join them.

"This is Inspector Sam Cobbs and her partner, Sergeant Bob Jones. They'll take care of you, Mark. I'll get you a strong cup of tea."

"Cheers, Helen."

Mark started to get on his feet, but Sam raised her hand to stop him.

"Stay there."

She and Bob pulled out the chairs opposite him and sank into them.

"What can you tell us?" Sam asked.

"I heard you had set up here. As soon as I spotted the body, I drove down here. Thought it would be better than ringing nine-nine-nine, especially as you're already in the area."

"You did the right thing. Can you tell us what happened?" Sam was already thinking two steps ahead. She'd need to call Des to get him and his team out here to attend the scene, but that could wait. Now she needed to know what Mark had discovered, and where.

"I was out in one of my fields on the edge of my land. As such, I don't tend to take water out there because there's a well nearby. Something felt off when I got there. The bucket was dangling outside. At first, I thought the kids had been messing around up there and had removed the bucket while they tossed stones in the well. It's not unheard of, little tykes will do anything for a laugh nowadays."

"But that wasn't the case in this instance, right?" Sam asked.

"No. I threw the bucket in and heard it hit something solid. Obviously, I usually hear the sound of water. I was distracted, observing my sheep. I carry out daily checks on them in case any of them are limping, so it took a while for it to dawn on me. It wasn't until I pulled the bucket up again that I noticed it was empty. That's when I took out my phone and shone my torch down there. I stumbled backwards when I realised there was a bloke in the well. I called out to him, trying to get his attention, but there was no response from him at all. That's when I presumed he was dead. I jumped on my quad bike and drove straight here, hoping that you'd be on site rather than canvassing the area like you were yesterday. You've been the talk of the village since you arrived."

"Ah, that makes sense. I'm sorry you had to deal with this. We're going to need the exact location."

"If you give me your number, I can send you a pin, which would probably be the best way for you to find it. It's at the top end of the lake. You have to take the winding road up there to get to it."

"I know the one. Don't worry." She gave him her mobile number, and he sent her the location. Sam handed the phone to Bob. "Can you arrange for SOCO and the pathologist to come out ASAP, partner?"

Bob nodded and left the table.

Sam smiled at the farmer. "How are you feeling now?"

He held his hand level, and it was shaking. Helen arrived with a builder's style mug of tea.

"Thanks, Helen, that's amazing."

"Don't mention it, Mark."

Emma arrived and asked if he was okay. "How are you doing?"

"I'm all right, Emma. Sorry for scaring you like that, coming in here like a charging bull on the rampage."

Emma patted him on the shoulder. "Don't worry about it. I thought Sam and her team should know right away."

"Thanks, Emma. I shouldn't be long here," Sam said and winked at her.

Emma took the hint and left them to it.

Sam let Mark take several sips from his tea. His gaze lowered towards his mug.

"When you're up to talking, let me know. There's no rush," Sam told him, despite her chomping at the bit to ask several questions going round in her mind.

"I'm fine. What else can I tell you?"

"Did you see anyone hanging around up there?"

He shrugged. "The usual walkers. We've never had any bother up that end of the lake, not really. Apart from the kids throwing stones in the well. I've caught the odd couple doing it and warned them off, but you know what kids are like, the more you tell them not to do something, the more they bloody do it."

Sam smiled. "Ain't that the truth? What about any other days this week? Have you seen anyone up there acting suspiciously when you've been tending to your flock?"

"I can't say I have. Not that I've been looking out for anything like that. I know you found a body at this end of the lake yesterday. That's why I came down here to see you right away. Maybe I should have stayed up there and ensured no one went near the well?"

"It's fine. Don't worry about it. When was the last time you used the well?"

"Two days ago. I usually top up the water in their troughs to last them a couple of days. I refresh it every other day."

"That's great. That'll give us a rough indication of how long the body has been down there. Do you usually venture up there at the same time, or do the times vary?"

"I prefer to stick with my routine. I go up there around nine once I've fed the cattle in the nearby fields. The sheep come next, and then I start on any maintenance jobs that need doing, you know, mending fences et cetera."

Bob returned to his seat and placed her mobile beside her. "All actioned. They're on their way."

Mark sipped his drink and continually shook his head in disbelief. "Why me? Sorry, that sounded selfish, considering a man has lost his life. Ignore me."

"No, it's fine. What did you mean by that? Have you had other issues to deal with lately?"

"Just the usual crap that a farmer in these parts generally has to deal with. I suppose it's the same for every farmer throughout the country. There's always something new we have to contend with that takes us away from our daily duties."

"I've heard it's a difficult life for many in the current climate."

"Too bloody right. Makes me laugh..." He fell silent and closed his eyes.

"Go on. I sense you wanted to say something important."

"Not really. Just what every other farmer gripes about these days."

"And that is?" Sam probed.

"The number of celebrities buying up farms just so they can get a TV show out of it. It sickens us. The reality is that being a farmer is a labour of love, with very little money coming in. You wouldn't think so, not looking at some of these 'celebrity farmers'. You know, the ones who have the TV money adding to the pot, enabling them to fork out seventy grand for a tractor. Makes me sick, it does. It's giving the wrong impression about how farms are run."

"I appreciate how difficult that must be for you. It doesn't seem fair."

"And now, my daily life has been disrupted by the discovery of a body on the edge of my land."

"I'm sorry. Hopefully, the pathologist and his team won't hold you up too long. As I'm sure you'll appreciate, it's imperative that we deal with the body as soon as we can."

"I know. Don't worry, I'm just venting, hoping that someone in authority will realise what we have to put up with. It isn't easy. None of it is, not these days."

"Why do you still do it, if that's how you feel?"

Sam realised she'd asked the wrong question when his gaze latched on to hers and he grunted. "Like I have an option. Nobody in their right mind is going to take on a business that loses money year after year. That's why I said all these celebrities getting in on the act is farcical. It makes no sense whatsoever. In my humble opinion, it's causing more harm than good."

"I think there are some authors who would agree with you. If you check out the charts at the moment, there are more celebrities releasing ghostwritten books than there are top-named authors."

"I suppose you're right. I've never really thought about it that way, until now."

"Anyway, I fear we've gone off track a little. Going back to the victim, I know it's asking a lot, but did you recognise the person?"

Mark sighed. "No, all I could see was that he had a thin patch on the top of his head. I'm presuming it was a bloke. I can't say I know many women around here who suffer from that problem. Is this going to take long? I've carried out what was expected of me; now I could do with getting back. Running the farm is solely down to me. Every minute of the day is accounted for. The longer I'm away from the farm, the more time I will have to make up this evening."

"I completely understand. Does that mean you're not married?"

"No. I had a fiancée once upon a time. She thought farming was far more glamorous than it really is. She left me three months after I asked her to move in with me."

"So sorry to hear that. I think we're done here. If I can take down your details, someone from the station will be in touch with you to arrange a suitable time to take your statement down."

He rolled his eyes and stood. "I suppose I should have expected that."

"Thanks again for letting us know as soon as you found the body. My team will venture out there now. We hope the forensic team won't prove to be too much of an inconvenience to you and your animals when they eventually show up."

"I thought about that. I'm going to see if one of the neighbouring farmers will take pity on me and agree to let me put my sheep in their field. They can be inquisitive creatures at the best of times."

Sam smiled and nodded. "That'd be great. We'll be in touch soon. Here's one of my cards, in case you need to speak with me in the meantime. If you could keep an eye out for anyone hanging around up there, acting suspiciously, I'd appreciate it. It's not uncommon for criminals to return to the crime scene."

"Really? Wow, you learn something new every day. It's been nice meeting you."

"You too. We'll be out that way soon."

He gulped down the last of his drink and then left the café, shouting farewell to Emma and Helen on his way out.

Sam and Bob went back upstairs, where she brought the team up to date. They left Claire holding the fort while the four of them set off in two cars towards the other end of the lake.

Bob's knuckles turned white not long into the journey. "I don't think I've been up here before. Watch out! This corner looks like a hairpin; you might want to slow down. There aren't many passing places as such up here, are there? How proficient are you at reversing?"

"I've heard it all now. I'm in possession of my Advanced Driving Certificate. You're not worried, are you?" She faced him.

"Keep your eyes on the road. It's too dangerous for you to keep looking at me."

"Relax. You might not have travelled up this way before, but I have, plenty of times. We should be safe this time of the year. It's midsummer you need to be worried about, when the tourists descend upon us."

"If you say so." He glanced down at Sam's phone, then at the pin on Google Maps. "The well is situated about a quarter of a mile from the car park."

"It shouldn't take us too long to get to the location now. I don't suppose you remembered to get a pair of wellies, did you?"

"Nope. I had every intention of doing that on the way home, except Abigail called me and asked me to stop at the supermarket to pick up some extra milk and cheese."

"And it went out of your head?"

"You've got it."

Sam breathed out a relieved sigh when they finally drew into the car park.

"By the sounds of it, you were as nervous as me," Bob said. "Go on, you just didn't want to admit it, did you?"

Sam grinned and hitched up a shoulder. "Stop whining. We made it here in one piece, didn't we?"

"Only just," he mumbled and flung open the car door.

Liam drew into the space beside her. He and Oliver exited the car and joined them.

"That was a thrilling ride. Glad you were in the lead, boss."

"I take it you haven't been this way before, either?" Sam asked.

Liam pulled a face. "No, never. It was cool, a white-knuckle ride, although I'd think twice about travelling that road in the dark."

"I agree. I've never been brave enough to risk it; however, Rhys has. I kept my eyes closed most of the time, pretending to be asleep."

Her three colleagues laughed, and the four of them made their way towards the location.

"Is it far, Bob?" Sam asked.

He glanced at the phone and then up ahead of them. "According to the map, there should be a large clump of trees over to the left. If I'm not mistaken, I'd say we're closer than you think we are."

Liam held his phone up and zoomed in with his camera. "I think I can see it. Yes, through the trees, towards the fence at the back." He showed the image to Sam, then to Bob for verification.

"Yeah, that's it, all right."

Oliver was carrying the crime scene tape. "We could zone off the area between the large trees at the front, at least until Forensics get here."

"Sounds like a plan," Sam agreed. "Can you and Liam sort that out?"

"Yes, boss."

Sam and Bob wound their way through the trees to the well at the rear. The area wasn't as muddy as Sam thought it would be, which came as a relief to both of them.

Bob turned on the torch on his phone and angled it down the well so they could both see what was inside. "Shit!" he mumbled. "Hello, can you hear us?" He glanced up at Sam and shrugged. "I thought it was worth a shot."

Sam nodded. "I was about to do the same. Maybe we should call the fire brigade. We might need their assistance in getting him out of there."

"I'd run something like that past the pathologist first."

"I'll give him a call. He's probably going to be pissed at me, but thems the breaks." She removed her mobile from her pocket, turned her back on the victim in the well and surveyed the surrounding area while she spoke. "Hi, Des, it's me. Before you have a go at me about pestering you, please, hear me out."

Des sighed. "Make it snappy. I'm driving. What's up?"

"My team and I have just arrived at the location. The body has been thrown down a well. I was trying to think ahead and wondered if you're likely to need the fire brigade to assist you in getting the body out of there."

"Hmm... are there any ropes attached to the body?"

"None that I can see. Nothing dangling outside, only the bucket that should be inside the well. I was thinking about the logistics of retrieving the body."

"Yes, I understand. Well, we're ten minutes from the location now. I suggest we figure it out when I get there. Whitehaven isn't too far away if we need to call in the brigade. I should think they could get to us within fifteen to twenty minutes. That wouldn't be too much time to wait for them."

"Okay. I'll leave it in your capable hands, then. See you soon."

"You will, if I can navigate this twisty road without having an accident. The fewer distractions, the better. No offence, but I'm ending this call now."

"I hear you." She hung up and then chuckled. "Another one moaning about how narrow and windy the road is."

"I'm not surprised. Hey, I suppose it has one thing going for it."

Sam frowned and asked, "What's that?"

"It's the ideal place to commit a murder."

Sam sighed and shook her head in disbelief. "Did you really just say that?"

"Sorry."

"No, you're not."

Liam and Oliver joined them. They tentatively peered into the well, and both muttered expletives.

"How are we going to get him out of there? He must be about twenty to thirty feet down," Liam stated.

"That's what we've been discussing. I think we might need the service of the fire brigade. We should wait on the track until then."

Des and his team arrived ten minutes later. Sam stood back, not wishing to crowd the pathologist. She pointed out where the well was and allowed him to make the call as to what they should do next. He returned to stand beside her. They both stared at the picturesque scenery in front of them and discussed the matter.

"We haven't got the equipment on board to deal with the situation," Des said. "Therefore, I declare your initial assessment should be acted upon. Do you want to call them, while we make a start before the area gets inundated with bodies?"

"I can do that for you."

"Horrendous, putting a body down the well. How was he found? Before you answer that, there's no smell coming from the corpse, so I don't believe he's been down there too long."

"The farmer found him. He uses the well to water his sheep. He confirmed that he uses it every other day. There was no body in it two days ago."

Des nodded as he contemplated the scenario. "Fair enough, that sounds about right. Yes, please, make the call, Sam. In the meantime, I'll get the techs to have a scout around for evidence and take the necessary photos."

"Leave it with me." She already had her mobile in her hand and rang nine-nine-nine rather than faff around trying to find the nearest brigade. The operator told her that they would be with her within fifteen minutes, and Sam ended the call.

She reported the information back to Des but kept her distance from the well. He thanked her and went about issuing further orders to his team.

Sam marched back to her colleagues, who had relocated to the edge of the lake. A couple of hikers, heavily loaded with rucksacks, walked past.

"Nothing to see here, folks," Sam shouted.

They waved and went on their way.

"Let's try to figure out the practicalities of the crime while we're waiting," Sam said.

The team gathered around.

"So, either the man was targeted as he walked, like Angel was, or he was deliberately brought here, either dead or alive, before someone decided to dispose of his body in the well."

"Are you linking the two crimes?" Bob asked.

"Let's say loosely, for now. As things stand, I think it would be foolish of us to dismiss that theory. Two murders in this beautiful area within twenty-four hours would usually lead me to believe there's a link. Although, we'll need to see what the pathologist has to say about it, first."

"They would need to have come from the car park, wouldn't they?" Liam asked. "There's a possibility that there's CCTV footage at the location."

Sam raised a finger. "Good point. That'll be your task for the day, Liam. There's bound to be a number posted up there we can call. Let's not rule out the possibility that we might be looking at two people here. They might have killed Angel and continued walking around the lake, coming here from that way as opposed to the car park we're using. The route is around seven miles. He, she, or they might have needed to take a breather, clear their heads after killing Angel, and then set off on a hike."

"And what? The urge to kill again emerged, so they thought what the heck, we might as well take out another fucker while we're here?" Bob said, venting his frustration on a nearby stone.

"We're just surmising at this stage, partner. Keep your anger in check; it's going to get us nowhere."

"Consider me told."

Sam stared at him and shook her head. "It's out of our hands at the moment. Once Des can give us a lead to go on, then yes, we can knuckle down and get on with the investigation. You know what it's like once a second body has been found. We're going to need something to link the two crimes before we throw too much time and effort at it."

"Sucking eggs comes to mind," he mumbled.

Sam elbowed him in the side. "Patience is a virtue, so I'm told. There's no point in us falling out about it, is there?"

"I'm not. I thought we were discussing the whys and wherefores of how two crimes of this nature could be reported within twenty-four hours of each other."

"That's correct." Sensing they weren't getting very far, Sam decided to go back to the crime scene. "I'm going to have a word with Des. You stay here."

She marched across the path and ducked under the tape to get to the well. "How's it going? Or is that the daftest question you've heard today?"

"One of them, yes," Des replied and grinned. "We've completed what we can until the brigade gets here. It's going to be tricky, getting him out without disturbing the body and any likely evidence the killer might have left on the victim."

"Maybe that was the killer's intention; to make our lives a hundred times more difficult than they usually are."

"You think it's the same killer?" Des asked.

"I was about to ask you the same question."

"Possibly. As we now know, the first victim's body was staged to look like she had fallen, which leads me to believe the killer is devious, intent on making us contemplate each of the crime scenes. This is a first for me, finding a corpse in a well. What's the logic behind that? Are we talking about an older killer or a younger one? One killer, two, or possibly a gang of them, trying to get their kicks somehow? Perhaps they're bored with village life and are keen to spice it up."

"Christ, I hadn't even thought about that. Do you think the objective was to get rid of any possible evidence? Is that why the victim was shoved in the well?"

"Your guess is as good as mine. We have no way of knowing what injuries the victim has sustained yet." Des glanced at his watch. "I wish they'd hurry up."

With that, Sam cocked her head when a siren sounded in the distance. "Not too long to wait now. Sounds like they've arrived at the car park."

"They should be able to get down here with their vehicle; the logging lorries go in and out of here all day long. So the signs say up on the main road. God, can you imagine coming across one of those on that narrow, winding track?"

"I hadn't thought about that. I think I'd crap myself and abandon my vehicle if that ever happened. Ah, here they come now."

The wail of the siren died as soon as the driver spotted Bob waving them down. The crew jumped out of the vehicle, and the officer in charge, and his second-in-command, joined Des and Sam.

It was Sam who made the introductions. "We weren't sure whether to call you or not. This is our dilemma." She pointed to the body in the well.

The two men peered over the edge.

"Damn. Okay, I think you've made the right call. We'll get him out."

"The thing is, it's important for us to preserve the body as much as we can," Des added.

"Don't worry, you can hang around and oversee the operation yourself if that's what you want?" the officer in charge said.

"Marvellous. Between us, we can get him out of there with minimal disruption."

The two firemen returned to the team. The officer in charge issued his instructions, and within minutes, a hoist had been erected over the well. Sam and Des took a step back, allowing the team to get closer to the site.

Des leaned in and said, "The only downside to having so many people here is that the scene is going to get contaminated and any evidence we might have missed will probably be destroyed."

"There was no other option open to us. The need to get the victim out and back to the mortuary should be the priority."

"Indeed. Let's hope we can find some incriminating fibres on his body."

The firemen made short work of getting the body out of the well and onto the plastic sheet the Forensic team had spread out on the ground.

Sam examined the victim from afar, until the firemen had finished their operation and gone back to their vehicle. "I haven't got a suit on," she apologised.

"I don't think it matters, do you? Not in the grand scheme of things. Don't get too close to the body."

"Can you see if there's any ID on him?"

Des's suit rustled as he crouched beside the victim. He checked the man's clothing and found a wallet in the first pocket he searched. "Ah, here we are. What will this reveal? His driver's licence is telling me his name is Elliot Carter. Well, get your notebook out."

Sam stood and removed her notebook and pen from her pocket. "Sorry. I'm ready." She jotted down the victim's name and then his address when Des supplied her with the information. "That's a start anyway. Thanks, Des. Can you give me a quick summary of the injuries and if they were caused by him being thrown into the well or not?"

Des glanced up and raised an eyebrow. "You're not asking much, are you? Let me have a quick look. There's a lot of blood on his trousers. To be expected, I suppose. Maybe his legs broke once he reached the bottom of the well. Hmm... maybe, maybe not. There are some marks on his jeans. Again, they might have been from taking the fall or..."

"Or him being struck by an object."

"The techs found a metal bar in the field behind us. We're going to run the usual tests on it to see if we can lift any fingerprints or possibly match the victim's blood."

"Sounds hopeful. So, by the look of things, he was beaten with the bar before being dumped into the well."

"Seems a likely scenario."

"The beatings, would they have been bad enough to kill him? What parts of the body were affected?"

"His legs for definite. That wouldn't have been enough to kill him. There's tape over his mouth, I assume, to prevent him from calling out for help. If he's vomited, then there's a possibility that might have caused him to choke."

"If that turns out to be the case, then what are we to glean from that? That the killer or killers hadn't intended to kill him, just leave him here as some form of punishment?"

Des shrugged. "I have no further suggestions for you. Hopefully, the PM will give us the answers we're searching for."

Sam ran a hand around her face. "Okay, we're going to leave you to it and start on the investigation now." She turned and made her way back to the rest of her team, but Des calling out to her stopped her in her tracks.

"Come back, Inspector. I've found something else you need to see."

Sam jogged back and crouched opposite him. Des pointed at the man's jeans.

"What am I looking at? The bloodstains?"

"Higher."

Sam examined the body again and this time saw the piece of material hanging from the belt loop of the jeans. "What is it?"

The tech fired off some photos and then backed away, allowing Des to remove it from the loop. "It's a handkerchief."

Sam shuffled a little closer. "What are the initials on it?"

"M and K. That's not right, if he's Elliot Carter. I'll bag it and do the necessary tests on it when we get back to the lab."

"Thanks. It does seem strange to have that with him. Maybe a girlfriend gave it to him as a good luck memento for his trip."

"Possibly. Bear it in mind when you ask the next of kin."

Sam got to her feet. "Of course. We're going to head back to The Gather now and start our research. If you discover anything else, will you call me?"

"You've got it. I'll be carrying out the PM later. I have a clear afternoon for a change, no reason to delay it. You never know what lies around the next corner."

"Speak soon." Sam headed back to her colleagues once more to find them deep in conversation about football. "Really?"

The talking stopped, and the three of them seemed embarrassed to be caught out.

"Let's get back to base."

5

When they arrived, Emma was outside chatting to a friend. She ended the conversation and waited by the entrance for Sam to join her. "How did it go?"

"There was definitely a body up there. We had to get the fire brigade to assist us."

Emma slapped a hand against her cheek. "Oh my. Do you think there's a connection to Angel's death? Or perhaps it's my furtive imagination getting carried away?"

"Possibly. Can you come upstairs? There's a bit more privacy up there."

"Sure. Let me tell the others where they can find me. Do you want a coffee?"

"You're amazing. I'm sure the team would love one."

"We would," Bob muttered as he swept past them and thundered up the stairs.

"I'll catch you up," Emma said.

Before Emma joined them, Sam instructed the team on what she needed from them. Claire was on the ball, as usual, and tracked down Elliot Carter's social media accounts within seconds.

"Makes interesting reading, boss."

Sam joined her. "What does?"

"He's got a few accounts, and without me carrying out further checks on him, they're flagging up that he's a tech entrepreneur."

Emma entered the room and placed the tray of drinks on the desk closest to Sam. "All coffees. You should have enough sugar up here already."

"Thanks, Emma. You do look after us."

"You're worth it, if it'll help you solve the investigation quicker. Can you tell me who the victim is?"

"We need to keep it quiet for now, so don't let on to the rest of your staff. We found the victim's ID. Elliot Carter. Do you know him?"

Emma sank into the chair beside her. "Yes, he comes in quite a lot. He sometimes uses this room to hold meetings with his associates. He's only been in the village about a year, but he's done such a lot for the community since his arrival."

Sam tilted her head. "In what way?"

"He's a regular contributor to every event we hold, whether that's at the school or within the village itself. He was determined to get involved from the day he moved in." Tears bulged in her eyes, and she swiped them away. "Why kill him? Jesus, he was such a nice man."

Sam rubbed her upper arm. "I'm sorry, love."

"Why? When is this going to end?"

"We don't know. Clues and evidence are very thin on the ground right now."

Emma glanced up, her eyes narrowed.

"What are you thinking?" Sam asked her friend.

"I'm just going over what I know about Elliot."

"And there is something bugging you?"

"Only that, like Angel, he was part of the book club."

Sam moved her head from side to side. "We'll bear it in mind. There's possibly another connection between the two murders."

"What's that?" Emma asked.

"They both liked hiking. Elliot appeared to be very fit, the same as Angel."

"Yes. He was in here only last week, making arrangements with Angel to tackle one of the Wainwrights together."

Sam's intrigue piqued. "Is that right? What else can you tell me about Elliot?"

"When he arrived in the village, he was married to Kimberley. She went off with another man, someone passing through, so I heard."

"Interesting. Does she still live in the village?"

"No. They moved back down to the north west. Where was it now...? Yes, I think Manchester was mentioned."

"Okay. We'll try and track her down. I don't suppose you know what her job is, do you?"

Emma shook her head. "Sorry. I haven't got a clue. I don't think she worked when she lived in the village. They had a red setter dog. She used to take it up the lake for daily walks, then drop in here for a coffee most days. She confided in me once that she found the house and the village somewhat claustrophobic."

Sam flipped open her notebook to check Elliot's address. "I'm not familiar with this location. Can you give me a rough idea?"

"It's between here and Kirkland. One of the larger properties that can be found down a lane. You can't see the house from the road from this end, but you can just make out the roof as you're descending the hill. It's supposed to have fabulous views of the lake and the hills surrounding it."

"I bet it's magical. Did he live there alone?"

"Yes, after his wife left him. He told me he was enjoying the freedom, the peace and quiet, and most of all, the solitude."

"By that, I take it he wasn't keen on dating anyone else in a hurry."

"No. Saying that, I think the door was always open to meeting someone in the future." Emma placed her head in her hands. "He was really nice, an approachable kind of guy. Not short of money, but he wasn't the type to flash it around either. Not long after he arrived, we had a bad storm that ripped the roofs off a couple of houses in the village. He was the first one to put his hand in his pocket as soon as he heard the two elderly owners were seeking donations."

"He sounds a decent chap. I promise you, Emma, we will get to the bottom of this."

Her friend smiled and turned to leave. "I'll let you get on with things. Give me a shout if you need me."

"I will. Thanks, Emma." Sam watched her go and waited until she heard Emma's last footfall on the stairs. Then she said, "There's one more angle I think we should look at."

"What's that?" Bob asked.

"The fact that both victims were separated or had broken up with their long-term partners. It might not be anything worth considering, but who knows in cases like this? I think we should bear it in mind."

"I agree, boss. I've found Elliot's parents' address and phone number. They live in Cheshire."

"Excellent, Claire. I'll call the local police and get them to do the necessary down there. Anything on the wife yet? I know she won't be classed as next of kin now, but we still need to check her out, just in case he was killed so she could get her hands on his personal fortune."

"She'd have to have a devious mind to contemplate doing that," Bob said.

"Well, someone had a motive for killing him. I'd rather do the extra digging now."

Claire handed her a sheet of paper. On it were Elliot's parents' details.

"Thanks. I'll get on this now. Are you all right, Claire? You don't seem your usual self."

"I've got something on my mind, boss. Can I get back to you about it once I've dug a little deeper?"

"Of course you can. I'll make the call to Cheshire." Puzzled by what Claire had just told her, she sat at a desk on the other side of the room and picked up the phone.

The local desk sergeant at Knutsford Police Station was extremely helpful. He told her that he would send a member of his team out to the address right away. She gave him her phone number in case Elliot's parents had any questions for her, then ended the call. Her gaze drifted back to Claire. The sergeant was typing frantically on her keyboard. Suddenly, Claire sat back and began nodding. Intrigued, Sam approached her and asked what was going on.

"It was a suspicion I had that I wanted to run with before I offered it up as a suggestion."

"Okay. By your expression, I'd say you've had some joy with it. Care to fill me in?"

"Well, it initially had to do with Angel's death, the way her body was arranged and the fact that she was found during a hike at the lake. Another thing that struck me as odd was that she was a fitness instructor."

"In what respect?" Sam perched on the desk closest to Claire.

"I recently read a bestselling novel set in that area, and the crime was pretty much the same."

Sam frowned. "A coincidence, surely?"

"That's what I thought, at first. But now, I have grave doubts."

"May I ask why?"

"Because of the second body showing up today."

"I'm not with you, Claire. Just tell me what you think is going on. I trust your instincts. I've never had reason not to trust them over the years."

"I'm furious with myself for not bringing the novel in with me. Off the top of my head, I think the second murder was of a man who had been thrown down a well close to the lake."

"What the...? Are you sure?"

"No, I'm not. There's a slight doubt in my mind about the order of the murders."

"If this is true, I find it incredible. Not that I'm doubting your word on things. So, what this amounts to is that we've possibly got a killer reenacting the crimes portrayed in a fiction novel penned by a local author."

"Yes, his name is Max Keane. There's more."

Sam raised an eyebrow. "Which is?"

"I ran his name through the system and discovered that he recently, well, two months ago, reported a robbery at his home, during which he was tied to a chair and possibly left to die. His cleaner found him a few days later."

"Where does he live?"

Claire jotted down the author's address. "I believe it's on the outskirts of the village. I've brought up his house on the map."

Sam stood to peer over her shoulder.

"It's around here," Claire said, "obscured by trees on two sides and at the end of the road."

"Out of the way. Was that why the burglars chose his property?"

"Possibly. I've got a copy of the book at home. I wish I'd brought it in with me."

"Can you do that tomorrow? It might help us figure out who the killer is."

"Yes, I'll bring it in. I wonder if Emma or a member of her staff might have a copy. It's called *The Truth Will Out*."

"You've been amazing. Bob, we're going out. The rest of you continue with the social media searches. Claire, if you can add Max Keane into the mix now, that'd be great."

Bob stood and walked towards the door. Sam hitched on her jacket and joined him.

She threw him the keys to her car. "I won't be long; I need to have a brief word with Emma before we head off." Sam entered the café to find Emma chatting with a member of staff about rearranging some of the stock. "Sorry to interrupt."

"I'll get back to you in a moment, Suzy. I won't be long."

The member of staff made her way behind the counter.

"Is something wrong?" Emma asked, her tone edged with concern.

"Can we talk in your office?"

Emma led the way. "You're worrying me."

"Something has come to light that I'm keen to investigate. I wanted to get your take on it before I visit someone."

"Sounds intriguing. If I can help, I will."

Once they'd reached the office and Sam had closed the door behind them, they both remained standing.

"A member of my team recently read a book based in this area by a Max Keane. Do you know him?"

Emma dropped into her seat. "Yes, I know him. Don't tell me he's been found dead as well?"

"No. Stop letting your imagination run away from you. So you know him? How well?"

"He's a bit of a recluse; however, saying that, he does attend the book club now and again. Actually, he recently honoured some members of the club by recruiting them as his beta readers."

"Meaning they're lucky enough to read the book before it goes to print, is that right?"

"Yes."

"I see. I don't suppose you have a copy of his book *The Truth Will Out*, do you?"

"I do, but obviously not here. I can nip home and fetch it for you if that's what you want."

"Only if you have the time."

"There's a lull before the lunchtime rush. I can go now and be back within twenty minutes. Do you think the murders are connected to Max?"

"Claire has read the book. She told me that the two murders have similarities to the murders written about in the book."

"Oh no. That's got to be an author's worst nightmare, someone copying the crimes they've invented."

"Exactly. Bob and I are on our way out to visit the author now. What can you tell me about him? Forewarned is forearmed, as they say."

"He's the type who prefers his own company. I recall he reluctantly came to the book club when it was requested of him."

"I've heard that most authors are reclusive and aren't keen on mingling, whether to discuss their work or in general."

"That's undeniable in his case. I'll shoot home now. Good luck interviewing him."

Sam grinned. "Thanks. I'm not sure what his reaction is likely to be when he hears the news. See you later."

Sam flew through the café and out to the car. She jumped into the driver's seat and backed out of the space, aware that there probably wouldn't be a free one when they returned. She glanced in her rear-view mirror and saw Emma getting into her electric car, probably sensing the same thing about her space.

The road Max lived on turned out to be far worse than the one they'd taken to reach the second crime scene that morning.

"Jesus, what is it with these narrow bloody lanes in this village?"

"Stop complaining. All you have to do is sit there while I do all the hard work, navigating the damn thing."

"I'm still allowed to moan about it," he grumbled. He crossed his arms in protest and sank lower into his seat.

"I wonder what sort of reception we're going to get from the author."

"No idea. I can't say I've ever spoken to one before, not in person."

"I'm intrigued to know what he has to say about all of this."

"I can't imagine him being too thrilled about it, can you?"

"You're probably right. It'll still be interesting to find out what his take on it is."

"Well, according to the map, we're five minutes away from his house. You wouldn't catch me buying a property out here, not in a month of Sundays."

"For once, I have to agree with you. This would be far too remote for me."

The detached cottage appeared in front of them. It had trees on either side. Sam strained her neck and caught a glimpse of the lake behind the property. "Oh my, now I'm here, I think it would be magical to live here and escape the world as we know it."

Bob glanced her way and pulled a face. "Are you for real? Living here would be hell on earth for me."

She shrugged. "Each to their own." Sam opened the creaking wooden gate and entered the small, neatly presented garden. She rang the bell.

It took a while for Max Keane to open it.

"Oh my, sorry for the delay. I don't tend to get many visitors out here. I thought my hearing was playing tricks on me."

Sam smiled and flashed her ID. "I can imagine. I'm DI Sam Cobbs, Mr Keane, and this is my partner, DS Bob Jones. Would it be convenient if we come in and have a quick chat with you?"

"Is this about the robbery I had a few months back? I was wondering how long it would take before someone from the station got back to me."

"In a way, sir. Would it be all right if we come in and speak with you?"

"Very well. I suppose you'll be wanting a drink, will you?"

"No, we've not long had one, but it was kind of you to offer."

He opened the door and led the way through the quaint cottage to a spacious room at the back, which could be classed as a conservatory of sorts.

"Take a seat. I tend to write out here in the summer, but it's far too cold in the winter. I gather a lot of inspiration from the view of the lake."

"I'm not surprised about that. It's incredible. How did you find this place?"

"It came up for sale about twenty years ago. I took a punt on it, as I thought it would make a perfect holiday home for my family and me. Sadly, not long after, my wife died."

"I'm so sorry to hear that. Was she ill?"

"Yes, liver cancer set in. They tried their best to save her. She went through one bout of chemo but couldn't stand the thought of going through it all over again. She begged me to let her go rather than fight the doctors for an alternative. So that's what I did. During the summer, we used to sit out there on the patio. She had a constant smile on her face as she admired the view. She was content enough to die here."

"How long ago was that, sir?" Sam asked. She struggled to keep back the tears and coughed to clear her throat.

"Coming up to nineteen years ago. I'd not long started writing for a living. This is an ideal spot for it. Tina was a nurse until her illness took hold. It was devastating for me to see her suffer like that. Why can't God just take us when our time is up? Why does He have to make people suffer and regret what their lives have become at the end? My mother also suffered with dementia at the end of her life... sorry, you don't want to hear about that. What can I do for you today?"

Sam sucked in a breath and released it, letting it seep between her lips. "First of all, I'm so sorry for your loss and also for the break-in here a couple of months ago. Can you tell me more about that incident?"

"Two thugs broke in and tied me to a chair. I genuinely thought I was a goner. I think they were looking for money, but I don't keep any here. I use the bank and have a few investments under my belt for when I retire. Let's face it, the state pension isn't up to much these days. Lord knows what it will be like in ten or twenty years' time for when the future generation retires."

"I agree. Do you know how the assailants got in?"

"I think I foolishly left the back door open when I let my cat out. Why would I feel the need to lock my doors, living as remotely as I do? It didn't seem to make any sense to me. Of course, after what happened, I keep them firmly locked now."

Sam felt sorry for him. "Do you feel vulnerable in your own home?"

"I wouldn't necessarily say that. I suppose I'm more wary, and being extra vigilant is at the top of my list right now. Have you caught them?"

"Not yet."

"Then why are you here?"

"I wondered if you'd heard anything about what happened at the lake yesterday." Sam's gaze drifted to the striking view ahead of her.

"No. What was that about?"

"A young hiker was found murdered on the track."

"What? And you think this has something to do with the burglary?"

"Possibly. Can you tell me what was stolen during the robbery?"

"In truth, I gave the officer a list of items that I thought were missing, but I've since found them. I must have mislaid them at the time. The officer who came to take my statement reckons that we'll never truly know."

"Can you remember the items on the list?"

"They were mostly related to my writing: a bookmark, a letter opener, and a journal that I used to note down future plots. One of the robbers rifled through my desk drawers while the other mongrel searched my office. I don't tend to use it much. I haven't really noticed anything missing in there, but I can't be a hundred percent certain. I've gathered so many knick-knacks over the years."

"I'm going to confide in you, in the hope that what I tell you won't go any further."

"Guaranteed. I rarely speak to other people."

"A bookmark was found with the corpse."

He closed his eyes and shook his head. "Don't tell me. You think it was one of mine?"

Sam scrolled through her phone and showed him the photo she'd taken at the scene. "Is this yours?"

He gasped and nodded. "That's right. Oh, shit. What does this mean? That the robbers have become killers?"

"Possibly. Either that, or they might have passed on some of your personal items to someone else, maybe to toy with the police. You write thrillers, so you'll have a fair understanding of how crafty criminals can be these days."

"I do. I'm mortified that they've used my possession and placed it at the crime scene. Hang on, you don't suppose their intention was to frame me for the murder, do you?"

"We won't know until we track the murderers down."

"I can assure you, I haven't set foot out of my house, not since the day I was burgled. My cleaner handles any emergency shopping I need. Otherwise, I do an online shop once a month, which usually sees me through without having to leave the house. I've always been content with my surroundings."

"I wasn't thinking along those lines at all. However, a member of my team raised a valid point today, and I wanted to come out here to run her suggestion past you and get your take on it, if you'll allow me."

"I want to do everything I can to help you, Inspector."

"Claire, one of my colleagues, is an avid reader and has recently read *The Truth Will Out*."

He beamed, but his smile quickly disappeared. "Okay. Dare I ask what she thought about it?"

"She loved it, only that's not the issue here. There was something about the crime that we attended up at the lake that resonated with her."

"I don't understand. What are you getting at?"

"More to the point, the victim's body was found beneath a ledge. At first, we thought she had fallen from above, but once the pathologist arrived at the scene, he confirmed that he believed the body had been rearranged. He rang me after he had performed the postmortem to tell me that the victim had been poisoned, which was the official cause of death." Sam watched the colour drain from his face.

Max held a hand over his heart and whispered, "No, it can't be."

"Did you have a murder similar to that in *The Truth Will Out*, Max?"

He nodded, then left his seat. "I'll be right back."

Bob leaned over to whisper, "Poor bloke. He looked frigging distraught to hear the news."

"Can you imagine what his reaction is going to be like when he finds out about the second victim?"

Bob shuddered. "I know how I would feel about it."

The conversation halted when Max entered the room. He handed Sam a hardback copy of the book in question.

"I've marked the particular passage you need to read."

Sam was a fast reader and breezed through the section Max had kindly highlighted for her. Then she passed the book over to Bob to read.

"Holy crap!" Bob said and slammed the book shut. He passed it back to Sam.

"That's unbelievable," Sam said. "I would say that the killer has carried out the crime word for word."

"I'm so very upset by this. To think I've put the idea into someone's head, only for them to go out there and commit the perfect crime."

Sam gulped down the bile rising in her throat. "I'm sorry to have to tell you that there's more to the story. This morning, a second body was discovered. This time the body was found in a well."

"No, no, no! This can't be happening." He placed his elbows on his knees and covered his head with his hands. "I'm not sure I want to hear what else you have to say."

"I take it this is also similar to a murder described in the same book?"

He dropped his hands and composed himself enough to reach for the book. "May I?"

Sam handed it to him and watched as he flicked through it to the relevant page. He returned the book and pointed out a passage she should read.

"Oh, heck! Yes, this is so accurate. Unfortunately, the PM hasn't taken place yet, so I can't confirm what the victim's cause of death is." Sam read on. "Although it's as the pathologist suggested might have happened at the scene. The victim choked on their own vomit."

Max shook his head, utter despair evident in his eyes.

Bob leaned in and whispered to Sam, "Don't forget about the handkerchief and the monogram."

"Bugger, I had forgotten it."

"What's going on?" Max asked.

"Tied to the victim's jeans was a handkerchief with the letters M K."

He slapped a hand over his mouth and let out an expletive. "This is unbelievable. I'm struggling to get my head around this happening. To say I'm shell-shocked would be an understatement. Please, tell me what I can do to help you."

"At this stage, we're unsure how to proceed. Again, I need you to keep this to yourself. The only links we have so far are that the two victims, apart from living in the village, both enjoyed hiking, reading, and were part of the book club in Ennerdale Bridge. Plus, both had recently split up with their significant others: Angel from her boyfriend, and Elliot from his wife, as they were separated. We're checking their social media accounts, hoping to find what else connects them."

"I'm at a loss as to what to say. The only thing that is coming to mind is that none of those scenarios featured in the book, if that helps?"

Sam smiled and shrugged. "These are the realities of running an investigation of this nature."

"Didn't you have another serial killer case in the village not so long ago? I think my cleaner mentioned it, and then I heard about it on the local news."

"That's right. Fortunately, my team was involved in the investigation. We pulled out all the stops to bring it to a swift conclusion. The killer was apprehended within a week or so."

"Do you think there's a connection to the ongoing investigation?"

"It's far too early to tell. Personally, I don't think so. I usually have a nose for these things. Forgive me, I haven't read your book yet, though I plan to rectify that soon. Perhaps you can tell us how many murders take place within its pages?"

He closed one eye and focused on a patch on the ceiling as he thought. "Sorry, I should remember. The problem is, I've been planning out and have just started writing another book in the last few weeks. Plots tend to get muddled easily when that happens. However, I believe there were four murders featured in that particular plot, unlike the one I'm writing now, which has around ten."

Sam smiled. "Is there a reason why you prefer writing serial killer thrillers?"

"I haven't really thought about it. I suppose as a writer, it keeps the adrenaline going throughout the novel. It keeps the writer on their toes, as well as the reader when the novel is finally published.

But that's by the by. What we need to figure out is how we proceed. Or should I say, how you're going to proceed now that you believe you've made the connection between fact and fiction."

"Good question, one I don't really have an answer to as yet. Unfortunately, the killer is craftier than we're giving them credit for at this stage. My team is doing their best, but as evidence is thin on the ground at the moment, the investigation has stalled slightly."

"I can sense your frustration. My detectives often suffer from that during my fictional investigations."

"Yep, I bet. Glad you're keeping it real. Anyway, I'm going to leave you my card. If you think of anything else we should know, please get in touch."

"Of course I will. Please, don't be strangers. I'm not usually good with people when they show up at my door unannounced. In your case, I'm willing to make an exception."

"We really appreciate that. We've set up a base above The Gather."

"Makes sense if the murders have happened in the village... and in quick succession, too, I noticed. At least I left it a couple of weeks before the victims started to pile up in my novel."

"The killer might be keen to get to their endgame."

He nodded and rose from his seat. "I'll show you out." Max shook their hands at the front door.

Sam left the house feeling an unusual sense of peace that she couldn't put her finger on. She liked Max Keane, something she hadn't expected at the start of the day.

"What did you make of him?" Bob asked halfway through the journey back to the village.

"I liked him. Actually, far more than I thought I would. You?"

"He was all right, I suppose, for a writer."

Sam chuckled. "Oh, Bob!"

6

That afternoon, when The Gather shut at four, Sam called a meeting with a few of the more concerned locals. Emma and her team helped spread the word, and Sam was surprised by the number of people who showed up. She did a quick head count of the people assembled before her and stopped at fifty. More people were arriving at the rear all the time. Emma was standing beside her.

"Should I start? Or leave it another ten minutes or so?" Emma asked.

"Time is getting on. I think anyone who intended to be here is present now."

"Okay. Here goes."

Emma raised her hand to silence the crowd. "Thank you to all of you for attending at such short notice. Let's hear what Inspector Cobbs has to say without interruption, folks. If you have any questions afterwards, I'm sure Sam won't mind answering them."

"Thanks, Emma. Just checking, can everyone hear me at the back?"

"We can, Inspector," three people in unison shouted in response.

"As I'm sure you're aware by now, unfortunately, yet another body was found at the top end of the lake first thing this morning. The details of the crime are very sketchy at the moment. I'll know more about the gentleman's cause of death once the pathologist has shared the results of the post-mortem with me."

"Can't you tell us the victim's name?" an older man at the front of the crowd asked.

"I can and I was about to do just that, sir. The victim's name is Elliot Carter."

Multiple gasps and murmurings sounded amongst the group.

"His is the second body found within the last twenty-four hours. This is not right, not for a village of this size. What are you and your team doing about it, Inspector?" one of the older ladies yelled.

"What we can at this time, I assure you. From what we are able to deduce, there are similarities between the victims. The first is that they both attended the book club held upstairs, here. The second is that they were both keen hikers. The victims died while they were enjoying their pastime. What I need to know from the residents of this village is whether anyone has noticed any suspicious individuals hanging around lately."

Laughter broke out until a man at the rear bellowed, "It's the bloody Lake District, a tourist hotspot, and we're approaching the busiest time of the year. Christ, if you're asking stupid questions like that, it's not surprising you haven't caught the suspect yet."

"All right, Will, less of the sarcasm, if you don't mind. The job of the police is hard enough as it is without you flinging unwarranted criticism at them," Emma chastised the man.

"That's all well and good, Emma, but I stand by what I said. This is the second spate of killings we've had in this area within the past twelve to eighteen months. We've never had that in our entire history before. Something has changed. It's up to the police to work out what that is."

"We've had an influx of newcomers moving into the village. Maybe the finger should be pointed in their direction," another man shouted from the back.

"That's bloody uncalled for, Albert. I'm still classed as a newcomer, and I've lived here five years."

"You're different, Dave. You've immersed yourself in the community from the start and set out to become one of us without much effort."

"Only because you welcomed me with open arms. Elliot was a good friend of mine. I showed him how to blend in with the community and, fair play to him, he went above and beyond to ensure he got accepted by the residents. That's true, isn't it, Emma?"

"That's correct, Dave. I was very saddened to learn of his death and informed Sam about the effort Elliot put in around here the second he moved into the village."

"It's heartbreaking that he's gone. He did a lot of good in our community, donating thousands to the school and other worthwhile projects in the area when it was needed. Actually, I have to say, he was always one of the first to put his hand in his pocket without much prompting," a woman in her fifties, wearing spectacles, called out.

"I agree, Wendy. The inspector and her team are aware of his kindness. It didn't stop someone brutally killing him, though." Emma winced once she realised she had let the cat out of the bag, despite assuring Sam that she wouldn't mention anything about how Elliot had died.

"What do you mean, Emma?" Wendy asked.

Sam reached out to touch Emma's arm and whispered, "Don't worry about it, leave it to me."

"I'm sorry, Sam. Me and my big mouth."

"We're waiting," someone bellowed impatiently from the rear. "What are you keeping from us?"

"You have a right to know the truth. The two victims we've found, umm... we believe they were both murdered."

The journalists started firing off more questions, one after the other. Sam glanced over her shoulder at her team and rolled her eyes.

Bob clapped to gain the crowd's attention once more. "Settle down, folks. If you want to get home soon, you'll listen to what the inspector has to say."

"We've been led to believe the deaths were accidents," another man shouted.

"I'm sorry," Sam said, "I don't know who told you that. As I said at the beginning, I can't go into detail about the deaths. What I need from you, good people, is to know whether anyone was up at the lake earlier today or yesterday, and if they saw anyone hanging around or acting suspiciously... If you want to stay behind and would rather speak with me confidentially, then feel free to do so."

Murmurings and louder voices could be heard for the next five minutes, but not one person raised their hand to offer up any much-needed information, which only added to Sam's frustration.

"I want to thank you all for attending this meeting. I'd also like to assure you that we've set up base here with the intention of getting to the bottom of this investigation as quickly as possible. However, we'll need your ongoing support to achieve that. If you see or hear anything untoward over the next few days, please don't be afraid to come forward and either speak to me or a member of my team."

Emma patted Sam on the back as the crowd dispersed before them. "Let's hope something resonates with someone while they're at home this evening, watching TV."

"Fingers crossed, Emma. We're going to call it a day now. We'll lock up before we leave and see you in the morning."

"I hope you can have a restful evening, Sam. Though I doubt it, knowing how seriously you take your job."

"Don't worry about me. Enjoy your evening."

Sam and her team ascended the stairs, switched off the computers they had running and gathered their possessions.

"Thanks for the effort you've all put in today, guys. You haven't let me down, not that you ever do. Let's see what tomorrow brings. Hopefully, something might click into place and get the investigation going."

"We live in hope," Bob agreed. He locked the door after the team left and handed Sam the key when they reached the car park. "Have a good evening, Sam. Try not to fret about the case too much."

"I'll try. It's never easy switching off when I get home, which is why I like to take the dogs for a run as soon as I get there. Rhys is usually up for it as well, after being cooped up in his office all day."

Bob shuffled his feet uncomfortably. "Whereas I go home and usually put my feet up in front of the TV."

Sam shook her head. "Why am I not surprised? Don't you even help Abigail prepare the dinner or do the washing-up after you've eaten?"

He grinned. "It has been known, occasionally."

"Christ, I'm glad I don't live with you."

"That makes two of us," he called out cheekily, then ran towards his car before she could lash out at him. "Have a good one."

"You too, you lazy git."

Sam tuned in to the local radio station on the drive home. The six o'clock news highlighted the investigation, although, to be fair to the reporter, she didn't mention that the two had been murdered. Sam felt bad for not calling a news conference yet and was surprised by the lack of reporters floating around the village. Now she understood why—if they were assuming both victims had died in separate accidents. She wondered how long that would remain the case once word got out about the meeting she'd held at The Gather this evening.

What if one of the locals has a contact with someone who works at the radio station? I can't worry about that now. I just hope the journalists stay away from the village long enough for us to catch the killer or killers.

Rhys pulled up within seconds of her arriving home. He kissed her, then asked how her day had gone.

"I'll collect Sonny from Doreen's and tell you all about it during our walk. Boy, do I need to unwind this evening."

"Me too. What do you propose we have for dinner this evening?"

"Sorry, I haven't had a chance to even consider that yet. Maybe we can take something out of the freezer when we get back."

"Or we could ring for a takeaway. We haven't had one for a few weeks."

Sam winked at him. "Sounds like a good idea to me. My treat this time."

"We'll see."

Doreen made a fuss of Sonny, then handed him over to Sam. "Hope the investigation is going well, love?"

"It's going, Doreen. Still early days. How has Sonny been today?"

"As adorable as ever. He sleeps most of the day and perks up around five when he knows you're due home soon."

"It's amazing how their internal clock works. Thanks again for looking after him, Doreen. I'll see you in the morning."

"Enjoy your walk, Sam. Try to use the time to unwind. Have you got dinner sorted? I've got some spare casserole if you'd like it?"

"You keep it for yourself. Thanks for the offer. Rhys has decided we're having a takeaway this evening."

"Ah, right you are. Enjoy."

Sam tugged on Sonny's lead, and they met up with Rhys and Casper at the end of the road. The evening was warm, making their stroll more enjoyable than the sodden one they had taken a week ago. Once they reached the park and were able to let the dogs off their leads, Sam linked arms with Rhys and asked about his day.

"I had a few tough visits today."

"Tough in what respect?" she asked, fearful of what he was about to tell her after the danger he'd recently been subjected to.

"Emotionally charged, I should have said. One woman, only in her early thirties, has just lost her husband to cancer. She is trying to raise two-year-old twins on her own, with no support network around her."

"Oh, how awful for her."

"I know. I struggled to keep it together during the session. I gathered a lot of information for her, including contacts I know who work for different organisations, in the hope that she would reach out to them. I'm not sure she will. She seemed totally overwhelmed by the situation."

"Was someone looking after the kids during her session with you?"

"No, fortunately, they were both sound asleep in the pram. My heart sank when she arrived with them, but they never woke up. Apparently, she had been walking around for several hours, trying to get them settled after a very restless night. They'd dropped off to sleep five minutes before she reached my office."

"Poor woman. That must be so hard to deal with all on her own. I hope she takes your advice and seeks help soon."

"So do I. She looked absolutely exhausted. She hasn't been sleeping because the babies have been keeping her awake. I advised her to take a nap during the day when the babies had theirs, but she told me it wasn't as simple as that because it was the only time she had free to clean the house and prepare their meals."

"It sounds like her days are full-on—super tough if you have no support to count on."

"Plus, she's having to deal with her grief after losing her husband of five years."

"And we think we've got it bad some days. It's shocking what some people are forced to put up with on a daily basis."

"It certainly puts life back into perspective, doesn't it?"

"It does. Who else have you seen today?"

"A man in his sixties who has been made redundant and believes his life is now over."

"Oh no, now is the time he should be able to kick back and enjoy life, especially at his age."

"You'd think so, wouldn't you? But no, again, he lost his wife only last year. He's been dealing with grief and depression since her death, and he thinks that's why his boss forced the redundancy on him."

"Hell, just when you need your boss to show you some support, he does that to you."

"I know. I told him he needs to find a club to join or to start a volunteer role."

Sam glanced up at him. "I know Muncaster Castle is always on the lookout for volunteers. I'm sure he would love it there."

"What an excellent idea. I'll call him tomorrow and suggest it to him." He kissed the top of her head. "Enough about me. How was your day?"

Sam sighed. "Another murder to deal with." She gave him a brief outline of what her day had consisted of.

He stopped and stared at her when she mentioned the notion of the murders coming out of the pages of a novel. "Wow, that's unbelievable, Sam. I bet the author is mortified."

They started walking towards the bridge where they had shared their first kiss. "He is."

"I've never heard of it happening before, but I'm sure it must occur quite a lot without authors realising it." He shook his head in disbelief. "My, oh my! Have you read the book?"

"No, not yet, although I intend to rectify that soon."

"Did Max tell you how many murders he'd created in the novel?"

"Four. He went on to tell me that the book he's now writing has ten murders in it."

"Bloody hell. It's fortunate the killer hasn't got their hands on that manuscript."

"Yeah, I feel thankful for small mercies. Come on, we should head back now. My stomach is on the verge of rumbling. Sonny, Casper, here, boys."

The dogs' recall was exceptional, which brightened Sam's day.

Rhys dipped a hand into his pocket, patted both dogs on the head, attached their leads and gave them both a treat. During the walk back, he rang the Indian and ordered the takeaway. The food arrived ten minutes after they'd returned home—excellent timing, as they'd both had the chance to change and feed the dogs their evening meal.

Sam poured a glass of white wine while Rhys dished up their dinner. They ferried the plates into the lounge and put on a Netflix film.

"To us." She chinked her glass against his.

"I hope you bring your investigation to a close soon, sweetheart."

"Thanks. I hope that's the case, too."

~

"ARE YOU READY? I smell another victim in our midst," the shorter one said.

They ran out of the house and jumped into the car they kept

hidden in the back garden. It had been a gift from a dying relative for one of them.

"Where are we heading?"

"I'm not sure. I think we might aim for the author's house again. What do you think?"

"Hmm... what would be the point of that? We're leaving clues at the scenes. I can't believe the police haven't cottoned on to that yet. They should have arrested him by now."

The shorter one shrugged. "Maybe they're not as bright as they think they are. Either that, or they know we're trying to pin the murders on Keane."

They drove in silence around the village until they spotted a car coming out of the road that led to Max Keane's house.

"We should take a punt on this one. Follow her. Do you recognise her?"

"Nope, do you?"

"She seems familiar, but I can't place her. No, wait, yes, I know her. This is amazing, better than we could have hoped for."

"What are you going on about? Who is she?"

"A journalist. She works for the local paper. She lives up the top end of the village. It's getting dark now. I think we should follow her. Hopefully, it'll be completely dark by the time we get to her house," the shorter one said.

"You're nuts. There will probably be other residents around. Why do we have to risk it? Especially after the inspector called that meeting today at TG."

"Because we're impetuous fools. Next question."

"I repeat: you're nuts. There's no way we'll be able to get away with this. I'm not sure I want to take the risk."

"Whatever. I'll stop the car, and you can get out. It makes no odds to me, arsehole."

"That's uncalled for after what I've done for you in the past."

"Wind your neck in. You're either with me throughout this journey, or get out and leave me to it."

"Bugger off. I'm in it for the long haul."

"Good. Now shut up and let me concentrate. I don't want to get too close to her."

"No, I get that. But if you don't keep up with her, you're going to miss the opportunity to take her out at the end."

"I know. Shut up."

They followed the green Audi up the hill. It turned right at the top and pulled up outside the detached house, which the driver knew belonged to the journalist.

"Get your mask and gloves on. Remember, we don't want to leave any DNA behind. That'll keep the police guessing."

The darkness fell around them. They left the car and snuck up to the side fence of the house.

"Let's go. She's faffing around, getting her briefcase out of the car. While she's distracted, we should take the opportunity to strike."

They used the shadows at the side of the house to disguise their movements. Luckily for them, there were no streetlights at this end of the road, something the residents had been complaining to the council about for years.

The shorter one shoved the car door against the journalist.

"What the fuck are you doing?" she shouted, surprised by the attack. "Get away from me."

"Get back in the car, or I'll slit your throat where you stand."

"What? You can't do this. What do you want from me?"

"Nothing... No, that's not quite true. Why were you up at Max Keane's house earlier?" the shorter one asked.

"Because he asked to see me."

"What about?"

"That's my business. I don't have to tell you."

The shorter one bashed the car door against the journalist's shins. "Scream, and I'll kill you, and then come back to murder your family in their beds."

"Just tell me what you want."

"Nothing much. I told you to sit behind the steering wheel. Do it."

The journalist slid into the car and stared up at them. "Why are you wearing masks?"

"Nosey bitch, ain't you? Put your hands on the steering wheel where we can see them."

She did as she was ordered, and her hands were bound to it by the taller one.

"Let's get this over with before someone comes out and finds us here." The shorter one removed the letter opener from their sleeve and sliced the journalist's throat before the woman realised what was happening to her.

Blood poured from the wound in her neck, soaking her white blouse in seconds. She tried to speak, but the blood bubbled on her lips until the fight in her dissipated, and she slumped over the steering wheel. Her head hit the horn. The two killers straightened her against her seat and ran back to their vehicle.

"Victoria, are you all right?" a man shouted from the house.

"What a blast! I enjoyed that one. Let's see what the coppers make of that," the shorter one said, reversing out of the parking space.

"Hey, wait! Come back," the journalist's boyfriend or husband called out, chasing after the car.

"He's seen us. We should go back and kill him."

"Don't be such a drama queen. He saw the car, not us. We're safe, for now."

7

Sam groaned as soon as her mobile started ringing. "I had a feeling I'd get called out tonight, which is why I only agreed to have the one glass of wine." She answered it. "Hello, DI Sam Cobbs. How may I help?"

"Sorry to disturb you at home, ma'am. There's been another murder at Ennerdale Bridge. I thought you'd want to know right away."

"Damn. You'd better give me the details and then contact my partner, Bob Jones. He should attend the scene with me."

"My colleague is on the phone to Sergeant Jones as we speak. The boyfriend of Victoria Langley, she's a local journalist, rang nine-nine-nine to report that his girlfriend had been murdered. He saw the culprits getting away from the scene in their car. They didn't stop when he called out to them. He was too late to save the victim." She gave Sam the address.

"Holy crap. If it's the same killers, they're either getting brave or reckless. I'll get changed and shoot off. Has the pathologist been informed?"

"Yes, he's already en route. I caught him before he clocked off."

"He'll be pissed to still be working at this time of night."

"You know him better than I do, ma'am. But yes, you're right, that's the impression I got from speaking with him. He was, shall we say, very curt with me."

"No change there, then. Thanks for the call." Sam kissed Rhys on the lips and ran upstairs to throw on her work suit.

He was standing at the door, her jacket in his hands, ready to help her into it.

"Thanks. Don't wait up for me. I have no idea how long I'm going to be."

"Drive safely. Don't rush back."

Sam slipped on her ankle boots and zipped them up. Rhys held the front door open for her and waved her off. She felt gutted to be leaving him. They'd been snuggled up on the couch, watching a detective series they'd both been looking forward to seeing when they had some spare time.

TWO PATROL CARS and Bob's vehicle were already parked outside the victim's house when Sam arrived. "Have you been here long?"

"No, a couple of minutes at the most. No one has gone near the victim's car, not until the pathologist gets here."

"Rather than stand around doing nothing, waiting for him to arrive, I think we should have a chat with the boyfriend. Is he inside?"

"As far as I know. I had a sneaky peek at the victim, from a distance, of course." He shook his head. "It ain't pretty."

Sam walked towards the car under the guidance of Bob's torch light. He flashed it on the victim, and Sam muttered the first expletive that came to mind.

"Shit!"

"I told you," Bob mumbled beside her.

"Let's have a word with the boyfriend." Sam approached the house to find the front door ajar. "Hello. Anyone at home? Can I come in?"

A tall man appeared in the hallway. "Yes, I left it open so you could enter."

Sam eased the door open. She offered up a weak smile. "Hi, I'm DI Sam Cobbs, and this is my partner, DS Bob Jones."

"Come in. I'm Jason Meldrew. I'm in the kitchen. Can I get you a drink?"

"Two coffees, white with one sugar, if you're up to it. Thank you."

He disappeared from sight. Sam and Bob walked the length of the hallway to a stunning open-plan kitchen, dining room and seating area at the back. The TV was on low in the corner. Jason switched it off with the remote and made their drinks.

"I'm so sorry for your loss. Had you and Victoria been together long?" Sam asked.

"Around four years. I was going to ask her to marry me at the weekend." He pointed to a small ring box on the coffee table in the seating area.

Sam shook her head. "Oh no, that's awful. Can you tell us what happened this evening, or is it too raw for you at the moment?"

"No. I'd prefer to tell you now because then you can hunt the bastards down. She didn't deserve to die this way. Have you seen her? That image will haunt me for the rest of my life, blocking out all the happy memories I ever had of her."

He stirred the drinks and then gestured for them to take a seat. Bob and Sam sat on one end of the corner sofa, while Jason chose the other end. He slid the drinks across the glass table towards them, seemingly unperturbed about scratching it.

"I know how hard this must be for you. However, the more you tell us now, the quicker we are going to apprehend the culprits."

"The killers," he corrected sharply.

"Yes, the killers."

"Victoria had to stop off to see someone on the way back from work. She arrived home about ten, I think it was. I heard a horn blast and raced to the door, thinking she might need my help unloading the car, carrying some shopping in, or bringing in some files she needed to study at home." He paused to look down at his clenched hands. "How wrong was I? I saw them. They were standing by the driver's door. It was open, and they were staring at Victoria as if hanging around to see her take her last breath. I shouted Victoria's name and stepped out of the house. I tried to run after them, but I didn't have any shoes on, so I couldn't get very far because of the gravel. I saw the car. It was a white Micra. It seemed to be a pretty old one. I'm not an expert on Nissans, but that's the impression I got."

"What about the registration number? I don't suppose you happened to see any of it?"

"No, I didn't. Not for want of trying. It didn't have one on the rear. That was my first thought, to get that written down, knowing the police would need it. Well, that and checking to see how Victoria was. I used my torch to get closer to the car and… I had to stop. I couldn't get any nearer. I rang the ambulance straight away. I don't know how I got the operator to understand what I was talking about. I was spewing out a lot of gobbledygook. Eventually, she told me to take a breath and tell her slowly what had happened. The ambulance arrived, but they refused to take her. They told me I should have called the police. I didn't know if she was dead or alive. All I knew was that she needed my help… or someone's help. I'm sorry, it's just so hard to get past that image of her sitting out there. I couldn't stay outside because my eye was drawn to her all the time. I came in, went to the loo and threw up."

"It must have been hard for you. Thank you for making the call. I have to ask: do you know who Victoria visited on her way home?"

"What's his name now?" He glanced over at the small bookcase and removed a hardback that Sam recognised.

She swallowed down the acid filling her mouth and accepted the copy of *The Truth Will Out*.

"It was this author. I'm not sure if you're aware of this, but he lives on the outskirts of the village."

"We are. We visited Mr Keane yesterday. Can you tell us why she called to see him?"

"She didn't say. It was work-related. She was a journalist. I think it had something to do with the recent deaths in the village. Are you part of the investigation team taking care of that?"

"Yes. I'm the Senior Investigating Officer on the case."

"Oh heck, is that what happened? The killers came after Vicky?"

"Possibly. What else can you tell us about Victoria's job? Was she an investigative journalist, or was it her job to cover every incident that is newsworthy in this area?"

"She was the best journalist on the paper. Her boss ensured she got all the 'meaty jobs', as he put it. I never dreamed it would end like this. How did the killers know? I only knew she was stopping off to see the author at around six, so how would they have known her movements?"

"Perhaps they didn't. Not if she was killed here. I think if they'd known she had a meeting with Max Keane, then she would have been killed closer to his property, not outside her own home."

"How do you know that?" Jason asked, his brow furrowed.

"I don't. I'm assuming that would have been the case. Has she covered any other cases lately that I would class as dangerous?"

He contemplated the question for a few seconds before he responded, "No. I can't think of any off the top of my head. She rang me during the day and filled me in on the investigation that was going on here, on our doorstep. I never imagined the day would end like this. If she was killed because of the career she had chosen... well, that's just sick! Everyone is entitled to choose which path they want to take in this life without considering this type of recrimination, if you get what I mean."

"I understand completely, and I totally agree with you. Had she mentioned anyone causing problems lately? Had she had any kind of threat directed at her?"

He picked up his mug, took a sip of his drink, and then shook his head. "No, nothing that I can think of." Car lights could be seen in the lane outside the property. He twisted in his seat. "Someone's approaching the house. I'd better go and see who it is."

"Don't worry, we'll deal with it. It'll probably be the pathologist and his team."

"Ah, yes. Does that mean she'll be taken away now?"

"They'll examine the area and take photos of the crime scene first.

It could be a few hours before they head back to the mortuary. I'll have a quick chat with them."

Sam sipped her drink, then she and Bob made their way up the hallway towards the front door.

"Poor bloke. I feel for him," Bob whispered behind her.

Sam turned and put a finger to her lips. "Leave it until we're outside."

Bob nodded.

Sam crossed the gravelled drive to where Des had pulled up. He was still in his vehicle, talking to someone on the phone. She had to wait several minutes before he finished.

"Sorry about that. I just got a call from another pathologist down south, wanting my opinion on a case. He rang during the journey, and I couldn't get rid of him."

"No problem. The victim is in her car. We haven't been near her. The boyfriend found her. The killers were seen driving away. No plate number on the rear of the vehicle."

"My, you have been busy, Inspector Cobbs. Any cameras on site?"

Sam winced. "I didn't get around to asking him that; I was halfway through the interview when you arrived."

"You'd better get in there and ask, then."

"I'll go," Bob volunteered and made his way back to the house.

"The victim's throat has been cut."

"Nice. The killers wanted to add an extra smile to her, did they?" He grinned.

"Not funny," Sam snapped. "I have some news about the other two deaths, if you're interested."

"Come to the rear; we'll have a chat while I get changed."

Sam went over the information she had sourced since she'd seen him at the second crime scene.

He slipped on his protective suit and listened without interrupting, for a change. "Sounds intriguing. What about this murder? Any idea if it was featured in the book, as well?"

Sam raised a finger. "I'll be right back. The victim had a copy inside." She passed Bob leaving the house. "I'll be two ticks," she called out as she entered the house.

She found Jason standing in the doorway to the kitchen.

"Come in. Have you thought about something else you want to ask me?"

"I need a favour more than anything. Would it be possible to borrow the book for a moment?"

"The book? Oh, Keane's book, is that what you're talking about?"

By this time, Sam had reached him. She followed Jason back into the room. He collected the book from the shelf where he'd returned it after they'd left.

Sam flicked through the pages to around the halfway mark and speed-read a few passages. The author had a way with words. Sam would even classify him as being wordy with his descriptions, yet managing to keep the story going. She ran her finger down the page, searching for any mention of the third murder. She finally found what she was looking for twenty pages ahead. "Can I borrow this?"

Puzzled, he asked, "Of course. But why?"

"I've got a theory which I need to run past the pathologist."

"Go for it if you think it will help solve Vicky's murder."

She smiled and left the house. Des was still at the back of his van, gathering his equipment together.

"Sorry to interrupt, Des. I've got the book here for reference." She opened it at the relevant page and read out the part which described the third murder, and in particular, the murder scene ahead of them.

"Wow! What the fuck is going on here, Sam? You don't suppose it can be the author acting out the crimes in his own book, do you?"

"Having spoken to him, no, I'm not getting that impression at all."

"Then someone is trying to frame him." Des said. He brushed past her to get to the victim. "How many murders take place in that damn book?"

"Four."

They reached the car, and he stopped her with his raised hand.

"Don't come near without putting a suit on."

"Should I get one?"

"I wouldn't bother. We're working in a limited space here." He strapped a torch to his forehead and examined the area.

Something glinted on the other side of the driver's seat.

"What's that?" Sam asked. "On the right, under her hand."

Des lifted her hand and picked up the item. "Well, what do you know? I think we've just discovered the murder weapon."

Sam frowned, unable to determine what the item was until Des turned and showed it to her. "A letter opener. You don't see many of those around these days."

"I think you should ask our author friend and see if he's missing one."

"He's already told me that the killers took it during the burglary," Sam agreed. She glanced over her shoulder, searching for Bob, who was talking to a member of the tech team. She crossed the drive to see him. "What was the outcome about the CCTV footage? Any luck?"

"Yes. I left Jason sorting that out for us. I said I'd drop back in half an hour to see how he was getting on."

"Let's hope we can get an ID on the perpetrators. Des has just found the murder weapon in the car."

"Clumsy of them, or was it? Did they deliberately leave it at the scene for us to find?"

"That's my take on it. I'm intrigued to see what's on the footage. We could run a trace on the car. I know we haven't got the plate number, but there can't be that many white Micras around, can there?"

"I wouldn't have thought so. I'll check how Jason is doing. I'm going to ask a really dumb question now. Just consider what time it is before you slap me down."

Sam smiled. "Ask away. I bet I can guess what it is, though." She waved the book in her hand.

"That's it. Why are you holding it?"

"Because I wanted to compare the crime scene to the third murder that takes place in the book."

"And?" Bob bit his lip, seemingly troubled by what the answer might be.

"It fits exactly."

"Holy shit! Another nail in the author's coffin."

Sam shook her head vehemently. "Sorry, I'm not thinking that way at all."

"Come on, Sam. I think you're wrong. He's got to have something to do with this. Don't get swayed by his charming persona."

Her eyes widened. "I'm not. I'm going on gut instinct here, and I just can't see him being involved. Don't forget, two people attacked him in his home. They stole several of his personal items, which we believe have shown up at the crime scenes. I truly believe they must have a grudge against him for some reason, and that's why they're doing all they can to set Keane up."

"I've got my doubts about that. It's too easy to blame others when it looks bad on yourself."

"We'll have to agree to disagree on that point, for now."

"Don't forget Victoria visited him before she came home tonight."

"I haven't, far from it. My take on what happened here this evening is that perhaps the killers followed her out to Keane's house, maybe not all the way, because they were aware of how narrow the road is. Perhaps they hung around, parked up in the village and waited for her to emerge, then followed her home so they could do the deed."

"Why not stop her before she made it home?"

Sam held up the book again. "Because the victim was killed in her drive."

"Shit! Okay, I wasn't aware of that fact." He kicked out at the gravel. "I'll give Jason a hand."

"Here, you can return it for me while you're at it."

Bob took the book and walked back to the house.

Sam crossed the drive towards the crime scene. "Have you discovered anything else yet?"

Des stood back, allowing one of his tech team members to take the photos of the crime scene. "Not yet. I thought I'd get the shots out of the way first."

"Do you need me here?" Sam asked, another idea brewing in her mind.

"Not really, no. The next few hours will be dependent on us examining the crime scene and taking the necessary samples for evidence." He glanced behind him. "It's not like we have anything to concern us outside the car. We're not likely to pick up any footprints from the gravel. You know how these things work by now. Why? What did you have in mind? Or is an early night calling you?" He smirked, teasing her.

"Hardly. I'm here for the duration, if I have to be."

"You don't. Do what you have to do."

Sam returned to the house to check if Bob and Jason had sourced the footage yet.

"Ah, there you are," Bob said. "Here's what we've got so far." He crossed the room to show her the footage they'd found on Jason's phone. He zoomed in using his fingers to tweak the screen and whispered, "The fuckers were wearing masks."

"I'm not surprised." Sam watched the couple run up and open the driver's door, startling Victoria. She got out of the car, and they forced her back into it, slamming the door against her legs when she objected. "Heartless bastards. They didn't show her any mercy, did they?"

"None at all," Bob agreed. "I'd love to get my hands on the bastards. To me, this was an unprovoked attack. She didn't stand a chance."

"Furthermore, they've got some gall, striking here, outside her house."

"Yep, that's what is bugging me the most about this pair. They don't seem to be worried about getting caught."

Sam nodded. "I agree. They don't seem to be showing any fear. Risk-takers in the extreme, killing at will, judging by the murders that have taken place already."

"What's driving them to do it? The book? The author?"

Sam blew out a breath. "I wish I knew," she replied, keeping her voice low so Jason couldn't overhear what they were discussing. "Can we get a copy of this footage, Jason?"

"Once I've figured out how to do it. I'll ring my mate, Scott; he'll know, but it's a bit late to call him now."

"No problem, in the morning will do."

"Leave it with me."

"We're going to shoot off. I'll be in touch soon regarding taking a statement from you, if that's all right?"

"I'm not going anywhere. Shit, I've just realised, I'm going to need to call Victoria's parents. I can't say I'm looking forward to that task."

"Would you rather I did it?"

"Thanks for the offer, but I think it would be better coming from me."

"I believe it would, too. Do they live locally?"

"In Workington."

"Good luck. We'll see ourselves out."

Once they were outside, Sam said, "We'll leave your car here and go in mine to see Max Keane."

"At this time of night? I wouldn't be happy if coppers turned up on my doorstep after ten-thirty."

"I don't care. I'm going. It's up to you whether you come with me or not. Or is it my driving that's worrying you?"

"Might be."

"All right. You win; we'll take your car. I can be the one clinging to the seat during the ride, for a change."

"Charming. I'm a safe driver."

She cocked an eyebrow. "I don't like what you're implying with that statement. Come on, we're wasting time hanging around here, arguing the toss. I'd like to get home before midnight, if it's all the same to you."

"Now that's something we agree on." He clicked open his car doors and said, "Your carriage awaits, ma'am. Umm... I should warn you, I haven't cleaned it out in months."

Sam turned her back on him and muttered some well-chosen

expletives. But when she reached the car and peered through the window, she realised he was winding her up. "I'll get you for that."

He grinned. "Just keeping you on your toes. Your chariot awaits, m'lady."

The drive out to Max's house did indeed have Sam clinging to her seat. "Slow down, you know how dangerous this road can be."

"It's fine. I know it like the back of my hand by now. You worry too much."

"I'd prefer to get there in one piece, if it's all the same to you."

Luckily, when they reached the property, they found the house still lit up. "There, my intuition was right, after all. He's a night owl and probably writes better at night than he does during the day. Umm... that is, when he's not interrupted."

"He'll be pissed off about us interrupting his flow, especially as Victoria has already visited this evening."

"We'll soon find out."

After they exited the car, Sam rang the bell. The door was swiftly opened by Max, who seemed perplexed to see them.

"Hello, Max. Do you mind if we come in for a moment to speak with you?"

"Inspector, Sergeant. What are you doing here? Yes... no, sorry, do come in. I must say, this is quite a shock, to see you on my doorstep at this time of night. Is everything all right?"

He took a step back, allowing them to enter the hallway. Bob closed the door behind them.

"Can we go through to the lounge?" Sam asked. "We have something to tell you."

"Oh no, there hasn't been another murder, has there?"

Sam smiled. "I think I should tell you when we're sitting down, Max."

"Can I get you a drink? Am I likely to need one?"

"If you want to pour yourself a brandy, that's up to you. Nothing for us, though. Not while we're on duty."

"This all sounds rather ominous. I'll give it a miss. You obviously want to get on with it. Come through."

He showed them through to the lounge. On his desk, the small lamp was switched on, giving him an extra source of light while he worked on his computer.

"Sorry, have we interrupted your creative flow?"

"It's fine. I can catch up with it. I was about to commit a murder, well, not me personally, the male antagonist in my next book. Enough about what I've been up to. Tell me, why are you here?"

He gestured for them to take a seat on the old Chesterfield couch. He settled into the winged armchair close to the wood burner that was giving off a subtle heat.

"First of all, I'd like to ask if you've had any visitors today."

"No one all day, not until Victoria, a journalist friend of mine. She popped round this evening."

"Was it work-related?"

"As it happens, yes, it was. I can tell by your expression that something bad has occurred. What's going on, Sam?"

She swallowed down the excess saliva filling her mouth. "It is with regret that I have to tell you that Victoria was killed this evening."

He bounced out of his chair and began pacing the floor. "What? I can't believe this is happening. Why? Why kill her? She wasn't like other journalists I know, which is why we had become friends over the years."

"I'm sorry for your loss."

He shook his head as if in disbelief. "She'd heard that there was a link between the killings and the book club in the village. She came here, interested to get my take on it. I was going to add that you'll be pleased to know I didn't tell her about your notion that the murders were being copied from my book, but I guess that would be inappropriate now."

"I see. Did she seem happy when she left?"

"Yes. We had a chat about other things while she was here. Like I said, she was a personal friend of mine. If she hadn't been, I doubt very much that I would have let a journalist into my home." He returned to his seat and placed his head in his hands. Suddenly, he glanced up and asked, "Does this have something to do with your investigation?" He shook his head. "Silly me, of course it does, otherwise you wouldn't be here."

Sam sighed. "Unfortunately, Victoria was killed with a letter opener."

He closed his eyes and groaned. He opened them again and said, "I'm sorry, I think I need that drink after all."

"Please, help yourself. We're not in a rush."

He got to his feet, unsteady this time.

Sam held out a hand. "Wait, do you want Bob to get it for you?"

He flopped into his chair once more. "Maybe that would be for the best, thank you."

Bob shot out of his chair. "Sorry, where do you keep your brandy? Assuming that's what you want?"

"On the side in the kitchen. I sometimes add a little shot to my coffee in the evening when I'm working."

Bob left the room.

"This is so distressing. I'm sorry if you think I'm overreacting to the news. Victoria was very special to me. She always treated me like a normal human being, rather than a nutty, reclusive writer, as most people in the village have done in the past."

"I'm so sorry. She sounded a wonderful lady. Do you think the letter opener might be yours?"

He left his seat on shaky legs to rummage in the desk drawers and then started tearing through the paperwork strewn across his desk. "I'll double-check it's not here. Sometimes, I forget to put it back in the drawer when I'm busy, but no, it's nowhere to be found." He flopped into his seat again as Bob entered the room. He took the glass of amber liquid from her partner and downed half the measure in one gulp.

"Take your time. We're going to have to examine the item for fingerprints to make sure it's yours."

"These bastards are doing this intentionally. They're trying to set me up for the murders. Surely you can see that, Inspector, can't you?"

Sam raised her hand. "Please, try to keep calm. I have no doubts about your innocence in this. I want to assure you about that."

He took another sip and sat back. "Gosh, I can't tell you how relieved I am that you believe me. I'm a novelist who happens to write thrillers in which people are killed. That doesn't automatically make me a murderer."

"I know. Please don't worry about that side of things. What we need to find out is why the killers are trying to set you up. Do you have any ideas?"

"Not really, no. I wish I did, surely that would put an end to these murders. There's nothing I'd like more. Knowing that something I created is causing all this murder and mayhem is, well, soul-destroying. I've been sitting at my desk all day, tweaking the plot of my latest novel, cutting out several of the murders, just in case it happens again. What if you don't catch the killers and they end up going through the other novels I've published over the years? That thought is constantly going around in my head. The problem is, I can't stop writing. I mainly do it to keep sane. I dread to think what state my mental health would be in if I didn't put pen to paper, so to speak. It's saved me countless times over the years from slitting my wrists. I know how absurd that sounds—someone who kills people for a living, on paper, being at risk of taking their own life. But it happens to be the truth."

"I'm sorry to hear that. Please, don't stop writing. Hopefully, this is a one-off. We're doing everything we can to track down the killers, that's why we're still working at this time of night."

"I appreciate your kind words and dedication to the cause, Sam. If only I knew why the killers are doing this, I'd tell you in a heartbeat. The truth is, I haven't got a clue. It's a bloody mystery to me. Can you tell me how they killed Victoria?"

Sam cringed before she revealed the truth. "The letter opener was used to slit her throat."

"Oh God! That's just awful. Where did it happen?"

"The killers must have followed her home. They attacked her, then killed her outside her house. Her boyfriend heard the horn sound. He came out and chased the killers off. The good news is that we've got their vehicle on the doorbell cam footage."

"Wow, the audacity of these criminals! Let's hope this proves to be their downfall. Do you know the vehicle? Is it locally owned?"

"That's what we need to find out. There were no plates on the rear, so we're none the wiser. We'll get the team on it first thing in the morning. It's too late to do anything about it now. For reference, it was an older model Nissan Micra, a white one. Do you know anyone who owns such a car?"

He chewed his lip as he thought. "I'm sorry, no, I don't. I'm not really a car enthusiast. As long as it has four wheels and an engine and can get me from A to B, that's all that matters."

"You don't recall anyone visiting you over the last few months in a Micra?"

"No, sorry. I've had very few visitors, and I don't usually take any notice of the car they're driving."

"Fair enough. Going back to your meeting with Victoria, can you tell us what the outcome was?"

"That she was going to run an article about the investigation, but that wasn't going to be printed for a few days. She had every intention of tracking you down to get your take on it before it went to print. She asked if I trusted you to do a good job. I told her I did, unreservedly. That you had showed me nothing but kindness and understanding throughout the interview. She was pleased about that. I'm devastated she's no longer with us, and I feel guilty that she was killed because of a blasted book I wrote. The killers must be bloody warped, have a screw loose, to be so vindictive, if that's what this is all about. I never meant for any of this to happen. I wish I'd never written the damn thing now. It's sold over three million copies since it was released, not that I've seen much in the way of royalties. People have a misconception that writers are wealthy. I have one answer to that: look around you."

"Sorry to hear that. Why do you do it?"

"As I said earlier, if I didn't write, I doubt if I would be here. Most writers I know, see writing, pumping out books, as a form of therapy.

It comes from within. They wouldn't be half the people they are if they didn't have that outlet available to them. Most of them, like me, wouldn't be here if they were forced to give it up. If it weren't for the greedy publishing houses taking their 'significant cut' from the pot, I think writers as a whole would be more content with their work. If that even make sense? It does to my ears, but then, I'm the one spouting the nonsense in the first place."

"Yes, it makes perfect sense to me. You've definitely opened my eyes about the publishing industry. Is it the same in the US?"

"Probably. Although saying that, the US market is a lot larger than ours. Therefore, the writers on that side of the pond are more likely to be wealthier than those living in the UK, due to the sheer volume of books sold."

"I understand. I suppose the American publishers can afford to spend more on marketing the books if the audience is there to tap into."

He pointed at her. "Exactly. Anyway, I fear we've drifted far off the subject now. Is there anything else I can tell you?"

"Not unless you can rack your brains and come up with a motive as to why the killers appear to be intent on setting you up."

"Believe me, I've thought of nothing else since you were last here and have drawn a blank every damn time."

"Okay, we're going to leave you to it now. Sorry we had to visit you to share such bad news so late this evening."

"I'm grateful you came out here to tell me personally. Thank you for that, Sam." He showed them to the door.

"You've got my number, Max. If anything comes to mind or if you sense you're in danger, don't hesitate to call me. Actually, it might be an idea if you stayed with either a friend or a member of your family, with the killers still at large."

"Nope. I refuse to let them drive me out of my home. I'd prefer to stay here. I'm on a deadline for my book, and if I don't stick to it, I get stressed and end up with nothing but blank pages. I don't think my publisher will appreciate me sending those in. Apart from that, this is the only place I feel comfortable enough to write. I've tried going on one of those writers' retreats with several other authors. Again, I didn't find it beneficial and ended up lacking inspiration."

"That's sad. All right, I can understand where you're coming from, but please, remain vigilant at all times and try to keep your phone with you. If anything suspicious happens, call me immediately, day or night, okay?"

"I will. You're too kind, watching out for me like this. I'm sure other SIOs would class me as a person of interest in their investigation."

"I think you'll find I'm very different from other officers. Bob here will vouch for me on that, won't you, partner?"

Bob grinned. "No comment. In all seriousness, Max, you're in safe hands with Inspector Cobbs and the team."

"Thank you. Knowing that will help me sleep tonight when I eventually get to bed."

Sam placed a hand on his arm. "You've had a shock this evening. Be kind to yourself, don't work too hard."

"I won't. Please, if you need my help, don't hesitate to contact me."

"Thanks, Max. Take care."

They walked away, and Sam heard the front door lock behind them.

Bob aimed his fob at the car. "He was shell-shocked, poor sod."

"I know. I hate leaving him out here all alone. This place is far more sinister at night than it is during the day."

"I agree, and that's bad enough in daylight. Do you think he'll be safe here? Are the killers likely to come after him again?"

Sam slipped into the passenger seat and rubbed her chin. "I couldn't tell you. Who knows what the killers will do next? That's why it's imperative that we find them."

"I won't argue with you on that count. Where to now?"

"Let's go back to the crime scene to see how Des is getting on. I'll need to collect my car, anyway."

"How long do you think we'll be out here?"

"Not long, I hope. Why? What are you trying to tell me? That you turn into something evil when the clock strikes twelve?"

He laughed at her suggestion and started the car. "You're taking a risk, winding me up when we have a perilous journey ahead of us."

"I'll shut my eyes, just in case."

"I should."

THANKFULLY, they arrived back at the crime scene in one piece. Sam told Bob to remain in the car while she checked on the progress the tech team had made.

"How's it going?" she asked Des.

He took a step away from the vehicle to speak with her. "It's going. We should be finished here in ten or fifteen minutes. Where have you been? Or are you going to tell me it's none of my business?"

"Not at all. We visited the author. Victoria had been to see him this evening, just before she was killed."

"Did he do it?"

"Don't be silly. We're searching for two killers. Or had you forgotten that fact?"

"I hadn't. Thanks for the unnecessary reminder. He could still have an accomplice working with him, or did that consideration slip your mind?"

Sam rolled her eyes. "It didn't. I'm a hundred and fifty percent sure he's not to blame for these murders."

Des raised an eyebrow. "If you want to be pedantic about it, actually, indirectly, he is. I shouldn't have to remind you that the killers are reenacting the murders from his novel. That knowledge alone should put him at the top of the suspect list."

Sam scratched the side of her face. "If you put it that way, then yes, you're right. But having spoken to the man twice now, I'm not getting the impression that he's hiding anything from me."

"Well, that's all right then. As long as you're satisfied, then that's all that matters during an investigation. Who cares what anyone else thinks, right?"

"It's late. Give it a rest, Des. I'm doing my best with the evidence that has been presented to us so far."

"Ah, here we go. I wondered how long it would take you to sink to that level."

Sam ran a hand through her hair. "Give me strength. I'm going to call it a day before we fall out with one another."

"You do that. On your journey home to your comfortable bed, you'd be wise to reconsider my words."

"Thanks for the suggestion. Let me know the cause of death as soon as you can. Thank you, Dr Markham."

"Of course, Inspector Cobbs. Sleep well."

She turned and walked back to Bob. He had the engine running.

"You're free to go. There's nothing more we can do here. I appreciate you attending the scene this evening, Bob."

"No problem. Did he have a pop at you?"

"I'm used to it."

"Chin up, don't let him get to you. I'll see you bright and early in the morning."

Sam gave him a weary smile and watched him speed away from the scene. She peered over her shoulder to see Des staring at her. She gave him an awkward wave. He responded with a curt nod. She slipped behind the steering wheel and started the engine. It was eleven thirty-five, which meant it would be close to midnight by the time she got home.

Rhys was in the kitchen with the radio on, stroking the dogs, when she arrived.

"What are you guys still doing up?"

"We were worried about you. I expected a call from you to tell me you were on your way home."

She kissed him on the top of the head and stroked the dogs. "Sorry, I thought about it, but given the time I left the crime scene, I decided against it. Come on, let's get to bed. We both have to be up early in the morning."

"Aren't you going to tell me what happened?"

"In bed. I'm knackered."

Before they switched off the light, Sam told him how her evening had panned out.

"Wow! Sam, this is getting ludicrous. I hate to go against you, but I'm with Des and Bob on this one. Maybe you should be regarding Max as the prime suspect."

"I can't. He's innocent." She placed a hand over her flat stomach. "I feel it in my gut. When are you men going to start trusting women's instincts? They're rarely wrong."

He leaned over and kissed her, then switched off his bedside light. "If you say so."

Sam sat there, staring at the wall ahead of her. Her mind was whirling, wondering if she was, in fact, doing the right thing, dismissing Max as a suspect. She turned off the light, but sleep evaded her for hours, the same question going round and round in her head.

No, I'm right and they're all wrong. There's no way Max is guilty of the murders... or is he? Am I the one who has lost the plot?

8

Sam drove into work feeling utterly dejected the following morning. She tried not to let her mood affect her during breakfast but failed. Rhys stared at her over the table, scrutinising her as if she'd grown horns overnight. She felt the need to watch what she said for the first time since they'd become engaged, triggering a doubt in her mind about their relationship. During the drive, she had argued with herself that she was guilty of blowing things out of all proportion.

"Hey, didn't you hear me calling your name?" Bob asked as she unlocked the door to the community hall.

"Sorry, I was in a world of my own. Nice to see you looking bright and breezy. I bet you slept better than me."

"Judging by your appearance, I'd say you're spot on there."

"I'll get the coffee on the go while you switch the computers on. I want to hit the ground running this morning."

"Sounds good to me. The others should be here soon."

"Exactly. I'll hold the morning meeting, bring the others up to date on the crime scene we attended last night, and then..." Sam said.

"And then?"

She sighed and blew out a defeated breath. "I wish I knew."

"Come on, Sam. This isn't like you. Not this early into an investigation."

"I know. I feel as though the world and his dog is against me."

"I'm not," he said adamantly. "If this is about Max Keane, all I was trying to say is that we shouldn't dismiss him. We should carry out due diligence on him, knowing what we understand about the murders and who came up with the plot in the first place."

"I know that. Seriously, if I thought he had anything to do with it, I'd bring him in for questioning like a shot. You know me well enough by now to know that, Bob."

"I know. It's a tough one. Sometimes I think we just have to take a step back and assess the information that has come our way."

She held her arms out to the sides. "Which is? Nothing of any relevance as yet."

He shook his head. She could tell how frustrated he was with her. Footsteps sounded, and the other members of the team all arrived at the same time. Claire narrowed her eyes, her gaze flicking between Sam and Bob. It was obvious she could tell that something was wrong.

Sam smiled and playfully punched Bob on the arm. "Let's start our day."

The team gathered around, forming a semi-circle in front of Sam. She divulged why she and Bob had received a call the previous evening.

"Holy crap! The murders are coming thick and fast now," Liam said, stating the obvious.

"You could say that," Sam agreed. "That's why we have to up the ante and capture the killers before they target another victim." She showed the team the footage Jason had given them. "Our priority this morning is to set everything else aside and find that vehicle."

A commotion broke out downstairs, and Sam rushed over to the window to see what all the fuss was about. "Shit! It's the press. Emma is going to be livid to see them here. I'm going to have to speak with them and tell them to back off. I half expected to be confronted by Victoria's colleagues today; I just didn't think it would be this early."

"Sam. I'm coming up," Emma shouted from downstairs.

Sam met her at the top of the stairs. "I'm sorry, Emma. There's been a huge development overnight. Obviously, the press has got wind of it. I'm going to talk to them now. Hopefully, that'll be the end of it, and they'll bugger off."

Emma frowned. "I can't see that happening. They're taking up all the spaces in the car park. There's no damn room for the customers to park their cars. Oh God, what have I done, allowing you to set up your base here, again?"

"Please don't say that. We appreciate everything you've done for us so far. I'll sort this, I promise."

"Not until you tell me what this new development is."

"You'd better come in and take a seat first." Sam hooked her arm through Emma's and guided her to a vacant chair in the office.

"I'm waiting," Emma said impatiently. Her gaze shifted between the other members of the team and then back to Sam, who had perched on the nearest desk.

"Bob and I were called out at around ten last night to attend yet another crime scene."

Tears welled up, and Emma shook her head. "What the…? This is getting beyond a joke. This person needs to be caught, Sam."

"I know, believe me. I've just said the same. We're going to be pulling out all the stops today. The good news is that we now know what car the killers drive. We have proof there are two of them, as shown in the footage we obtained from the crime scene. It's an older model white Nissan Micra. I don't suppose you happen to know who drives one in the village or possibly in the surrounding area, do you?"

Car horns beeped downstairs, distracting Emma. "No, I can't recall seeing one in the village, but I don't tend to take notice of the cars people drive, sorry. Who was the victim?"

"A journalist who lives in the village, Victoria Langley. Do you know her?"

Emma slapped a hand against her cheek. "Yes, I know her. She's not like the others. I always got on well with her. She and Jason used to come in here every Saturday for breakfast before heading up to the lake for a walk. What the hell is going on here, Sam?"

"I really don't know. Does she have a connection with the other victims? Did she attend the book club or go on hikes with the others?"

Emma thought for a moment or two and then shook her head. "I don't think so. I'll have to run it past the rest of the team. Would that be all right? Can I tell them who the victim is?"

"Yes, it's obvious by what's going on downstairs that the news is already out. I'm so sorry to inconvenience you like this. They're after blood. At least, that's what it sounds like. I'll hold a brief conference, and that should satisfy them enough to make them leave."

"Do your best, Sam, that's all I can ask. I hate bloody journalists more than I hate spiders and snakes."

Sam smiled. Emma stood, and they hugged.

"Leave it with me. I'll get them shifted before the café opens at ten."

"Thanks."

Sam and Emma walked down the stairs arm in arm and parted at the exit. Sam marched towards the crowd of journalists. They rushed forward, almost knocking her off balance. She held up her hands and pushed the men away.

Bob came hurtling from behind her and helped shove the journalists back. "Stop it! Inspector Cobbs has every intention of speaking to you. However, she will refuse to do so if you continue to behave like a pack of wolves. In other words, give it a bloody rest, or we'll be forced to arrest the lot of you. The choice is yours."

The enthusiastic crowd calmed down, and the journalists started firing questions one after the other. Sam's head was spinning. She refused to answer any of them because she couldn't make out what they were saying, as each was eager to make their voice heard above their colleagues'. She shook her head and walked back towards the stairs.

"Are you all right?" Bob asked. "Has anyone hurt you?"

"No, I'm fine. They're too much, Bob. I can't deal with them until they calm down."

Bob shouted up the stairs for Oliver and Liam to join them. They appeared swiftly, and with her three colleagues taking up a don't-mess-with-me stance, arms folded and meaning business, she felt safe to carry on. Sam remained where she was and addressed the crowd.

"I'm only going to hold a brief conference, then you're going to disperse and let the café open for business. Emma and her team can do without this type of disruption, got that?"

"What can you tell us about Victoria's death, Inspector?" one of the journalists at the front shouted.

"As you will already know by now, Victoria was sadly killed last night. We're aware of the vehicle involved, and we're doing our very best to trace it. Unfortunately, that's all I can give you at this early stage, so I'm afraid you've had a wasted trip if you expected me to reveal more. The truth is, there's nothing more available at the moment, for anyone. The post-mortem will be performed today, and until I have the results in my hand, I won't be able to tell you what the cause of death was."

"Don't give us that bullshit, Inspector. We've already heard that the killer sliced her throat open. What we want to know is whether her murder is linked to the other two murders that you're investigating this week," another journalist shouted, his expression set with grim determination.

"I've told you all we know. Unless we discover any evidence connecting the three murders, we don't feel confident enough to tell you or anyone else that they were committed by the same person or persons. You know how difficult a murder case can be. It's only been a few days since the first murder was carried out, and here you are, expecting me to tell you that we have a suspect in mind and that we're closing in on them, when nothing could be further from the truth."

Several of the men standing in the front looked at her suspiciously through narrowed eyes.

Another journalist, situated in the middle of the crowd, chose to challenge her further. "What utter tosh. Don't try to fool us into believing you don't know what the links are between the three murders, Inspector. Come on, you have to give us something."

"Do I? What do you want me to do? Make up a pack of lies just so you have something to print or put out on the afternoon news bulletin? It doesn't work that way. You know as well as I do that without concrete evidence to go on, an investigation can crumble just like that." She clicked her thumb and forefinger together. "I'm asking you to give us the breathing space we need to get on with our job. Right now, your distraction has drawn me away from my morning meeting with my team. Now, if you'll excuse me, I owe it to the families of the victims to get back to the investigation. You'll be the first to know if and when we find anything of substance to go on, believe me."

"Bullshit," mumbled a couple of the journalists who were standing close to her.

"I'm asking you to leave the car park. Any vehicles left here after this meeting has concluded will be towed away before the café opens. You have no right leaving your cars here if you're not going to use the facilities. If you do want to use the café, I'm asking you not to hound the staff. They know nothing. They are not part of this investigation. Emma has kindly allowed us to set up a temporary base here, and that can and will be rescinded if you cause any trouble for us. Am I making myself clear?"

The crowd dispersed. A few of them drove off, and the others relocated to have a chinwag at the bottom of the drive.

"I'm giving you ten minutes to move your vehicles before I make the call to get them towed away," Sam shouted the reminder.

"Yeah, we heard you the first time," a snarky retort filtered back.

"Come on, Sam. Let's leave them to it. We'll keep an eye on the time and get them shifted before the café opens," Bob said.

The four of them returned to their temporary office.

Sam sipped at her lukewarm coffee and grimaced. "I can understand their need to get to the bottom of what went on last night, but until we know the ins and outs of what happened, they're going to have to wait before the information can be put out there."

"They're not known for their patience, we're all aware of that," Bob said.

"True enough. Okay, let's get back to it, folks. Let's concentrate on finding this white Micra."

"Claire, can I have another look at the book, please?" Sam asked.

Claire reached behind her to the shelf where she'd placed the book for safekeeping and handed it to Sam.

She flicked through it to where the fourth murder was featured. "Great, the next murder takes place in someone's garden. There's no way we will be able to prevent that from happening. Therefore, it's imperative we find the Micra ASAP."

The team got cracking on the task, and Sam moved over to the window to check if the journalists had dispersed yet. To her amazement, they had.

"Thank God for that," she mumbled.

Bob joined her. "I take it they've gone now?"

"They have. I'm going to nip downstairs and apologise to Emma for their crass behaviour. Hopefully, it'll mend the bridge between us."

"You're talking twaddle. She was fine—same old Emma. She loves us being here, most of the time."

"I doubt if that's true. I won't be long. When I get back, be ready to shoot off."

He tilted his head. "Where are we going?"

"I think we should go back to the crime scene and see if the neighbours saw or heard anything that might help us. It was too late for us to start knocking on doors last night. Our luck might change. One of them might have got a better view of the car, or even the killers, on their doorbell cameras or CCTV."

"I'm with you, that's a fair point. I'll oversee things here until you get back."

Sam smiled and ran down the stairs to talk to Emma. When she entered the café, the staff were all gathered around, including her dear friend. The conversation stopped when they saw Sam. She felt uncomfortable the second everyone turned her way.

"Is everything all right? I'm sorry about the journos. I've given them what they wanted and sent them on their way. They shouldn't bother you any more, although I can't promise that will be the case. Why am I getting the impression I've walked in on something here?"

"You'd better come through to my office, Sam," Emma said before she addressed her colleagues. "Is everything set up, ready to open, ladies?"

"I've just got to chop some salad and we're good to go," Helen flung over her shoulder as she walked behind the counter.

Sam wandered into the office behind Emma. "You're not going to kick us out, are you? I can't apologise enough for them making a nuisance of themselves."

"Sit down, Sam. I have something to tell you." Emma cleared the spare chair of the books she'd just had delivered.

"Okay, I'm sitting. What's wrong?" Sam asked, her pulse racing and the adrenaline pumping around her body.

"Wait there. I need to ask Suzy if she can spare us a minute." Emma went to the door and called for the member of staff to join them. "I need to get another chair."

"There's no need, Suzy can have mine," Sam jumped out of her seat and leaned against the wall between Emma and the newcomer. "What's going on?"

Suzy sat in the chair and fidgeted for a few seconds, her gaze flicking between Sam and Emma.

"Tell her," Emma prompted.

Suzy tipped her head back and blew out a breath. "I really don't know how to put it into words."

"Just say it. If it comes out wrong, we'll figure it out together," Sam replied.

"Emma mentioned you were on the lookout for a white Nissan Micra," Suzy said.

Sam nodded. "That's right. Do you know who it might belong to?"

"A member of staff has access to one now and again, but I'm reluctant to say because I wouldn't want her to get into trouble. What if I'm wrong? She'd never forgive me if she knew I had dropped her in it."

"Just tell her," Emma urged. "Sam's not going to solve the investigation if people keep important facts from her, is she?"

"Don't get angry with me, Emma. This is difficult enough as it is."

"She's not getting angry, Suzy. We all want to get to the bottom of this as quickly as possible. We can't do that alone; we need help from the public. Come on, the floor is yours. Who is it?"

Suzy bowed her head and chewed the inside of her mouth for a moment or two. She raised her head again and whispered, "It's Grace."

Sam frowned as she trawled her memory for the woman concerned. *Grace? Isn't she the one who was comparing tattoos with Bob? Or am I mistaken?*

"Sam, are you all right?" Emma asked.

"Is Grace the one who recently had the new tattoo?"

Emma and Suzy both nodded.

"That's right," Emma said. "God, I hope Suzy is wrong about her. I'll be mortified if she turns out to be the killer. She's such an asset to the café. She's been through a tough time lately. Her father died about eighteen months ago. I suppose she hasn't been the same since."

"Hang on a second. What makes you think it's her? Apart from the fact that she drives a Nissan now and again?"

"I noticed she's been acting kind of weird during her shifts the past few days," Suzy told them.

"Weird? In what respect?"

"I don't know. Since you arrived, she seems to be constantly on tenterhooks. I've had to pick her up about a few orders that she has got wrong lately. That's not like her at all."

"I concur. She's usually the ultimate professional," Emma said. "God, I hope you're wrong about this, Suzy. Although I totally understand why you're saying what you are. You know her better than most of us. You share several shifts together. If you've seen a change in her demeanour recently, then Sam has a right to know."

"Don't worry. I won't tell her that you told me," Sam said. "I'll have a chat with her and tell her that I've interviewed the rest of the staff today, how's that? It'll avoid any suspicion on her part. I take it she's not here today?"

"No, she's on a day off," Emma confirmed. "I can't bear the thought of it being her, but then, who knows how grief affects some people?"

"That's true. Who do you think her accomplice could be? Because we're searching for two killers, not just one."

"What about Harry, her boyfriend?" Suzy asked Emma.

Emma sighed. "It's a possibility. She hasn't been with him that long, only a couple of months. He seems a nice enough young man..."

"Again, I've had my doubts about him for a while. I hope I'm doing the right thing pointing you in Grace's direction. What if she finds out it's me and comes after me and my family? I couldn't cope if I lost one of my kids. No, forget I said anything. I've changed my mind, thought better of it. I don't want this to come back and bite me in the arse," Suzy said, distraught.

Sam raised her hand to calm the woman down. "Please, don't feel bad. If you're wrong, then fine. No one will know the information came from you, I promise. Do either of you know what her plans are for today? Where I'm likely to find her?"

"I think she was going shopping in Workington with her mother," Suzy said. "They're sorting out a gravestone for her father's grave. Money has been short for her and her mother since her father passed away. She told me the other day that the life insurance had finally come through and that was how they planned to spend some of it."

"That's brilliant. Emma, can you give me her address? We'll call round to see her later, when she gets back."

Emma jotted down the address on a clean piece of paper. "Do you want Harry's address as well? Just in case she's over at his place with him. I think he's in between jobs at the moment."

Sam mentally pieced some of the jigsaw together. The first two murders had been committed during the day. "Umm... did Grace work on Monday?"

Emma checked the rota on the wall beside her. "No, she was off. Shit! That's when Angel was killed, wasn't it?"

"It was. Plus, we don't know how long Elliot was down that well. For all we know, they might have killed Angel and then gone for a hike around the lake and stumbled across Elliot. Perhaps their adrenaline was in full flow, and they chose to kill again."

Emma gasped. "This is unbelievable. What do we do now?"

"Who else knows about this?" Sam asked, her gaze locked with Suzy's.

"I haven't told anyone. It took an almighty effort to pluck up the courage to voice my concerns to Emma. I still feel like I'm betraying her, going behind her back like this. Maybe I should have come right out and confronted her."

"No, I would always advise against doing that, especially if she turns out to be the killer," Sam replied. "You've done the right thing, confiding in Emma first and then coming to me."

"I hope so. I'd better get back to work." Suzy smiled warily and left the office.

Sam flopped into the vacant chair and put her head in her hands. "I'm sorry it's come to this, Emma. You obviously know her really well. Did you have any inclination at all?"

"No idea whatsoever. Suzy is right. Now that I've had time to consider it, she has been... I suppose, anxious since you arrived."

"That's what we usually judge a suspect by: whether their character changes. Do you need a hug?"

They stood and embraced each other tightly. They parted, and Sam pecked her on the cheek.

"I'll get the team to search her social media accounts and see what else we can find out about her. One last question: does she belong to the book club?"

"Yes, she does. I believe she joined about three months ago. Actually, it was when Max Keane came to do a book signing and held a Q and A session with him afterwards."

"Did you attend that meeting?"

"I caught the tail end of it."

"Did you notice how Grace was with Max?"

"I can't say I noticed, sorry."

"Are you aware that Max's cottage was broken into two months ago?"

"Yes, I'd heard the rumours." Emma appeared puzzled by the question.

"I'm pushing your memory here. Can you tell me if the Q and A session was held before or after the break-in?"

Emma sucked in a breath and bit down on her bottom lip. "I can't remember. It's so annoying. It's this damn menopause. I've got a brain like a sieve nowadays."

Sam waved away her apology. "Don't worry. I appreciate everything you've told us and also your encouragement for Suzy to come forward. I'll let you know how we get on. If by any chance Grace drops in today, will you give me a call?"

"Of course I will. God, I hope she doesn't. I dread to think how Suzy and I will react towards her, knowing what she might have done."

"You can't react. It'll give the game away that we're on to her."

"What a terrible situation to find ourselves in."

"Don't worry. We're going to do what we can to talk to Grace and her boyfriend soon." She waved the sheet of paper with Grace's and Harry's addresses on. "Stay strong. I realise how difficult this is for you."

Emma leaned back and rested her hands on her head. "To say my mind is blown would be an understatement. I hope that when word gets out about this, it doesn't prove detrimental to the business. We had our best year last year. I'd hate to see all our hard work unravel because of this and Grace's association to the café."

"Don't worry. I'm sure it won't affect your business. The customers love coming here, and all your staff are warm and welcoming."

"With a smattering of serial killer thrown into the mix."

Sam cringed. "I'm going before this conversation deteriorates further. Stop overthinking things. That's my final word on the matter, okay?"

"Yes, Inspector Cobbs."

Sam winked at her friend and left the office. Suzy glanced up from the coffee she was pouring for a customer and spilt some of it on the counter.

"Take care, Suzy. It'll all turn out for the best."

Suzy nodded and fetched a cloth to wipe up the spillage.

Sam took the stairs two at a time. "You'll never guess in a million years what I've just learned," she shouted as soon as she entered the room.

"You've been told who owns the Micra and you now know who the killer is," Bob said. He crossed his arms and sat back in his chair.

Sam's eyes widened, and she asked, "Have you been spying on me?"

He sat upright and stared at her. "Don't tell me I'm right."

"You are. Go on, guess who it is?"

He shrugged and glanced around the room at the others. "I haven't got the foggiest... no, it's not Squeaky-Clean Emma, is it?"

She took a swipe at his arm. "Don't be so ridiculous. Try Grace, the girl you were comparing tattoos with the other day."

"You're kidding me? No way. I would never have suspected her. Is the Micra hers?"

"She has access to it. What have you discovered about the number of Micras in this area?"

"There are only a couple," Claire replied. "Both of them belong to people in their sixties."

"Might be her grandmother's car, or possibly the boyfriend's grandparents'. Either way, have you got the addresses, Claire?"

"I have."

Claire handed Sam the details, and she compared them to the addresses Emma had given her for Grace and Harry.

"Hmm... they're not a match to what I have. Never mind, at least now we've got a lead to go on. Emma told me Grace is out shopping with her mother for a headstone for her father. He died about eighteen months ago."

"Do you think that's the trigger for the murders?" Oliver asked. He tapped his biro on his cheek.

"It might well be. Good thinking. Let's do the necessary digging into Grace and her boyfriend. Bob, we should head off. I still want to see what the neighbours have to say about the events from last night. Hopefully, we won't be long, folks. Please keep digging."

They set off and arrived at the location ten minutes later. Jason's car was sitting on the drive. Sam felt the urge to check on him. She rang the bell. He opened the door, unshaven, with his hair sticking out at multiple angles.

"Sorry to disturb you, Jason. I just wondered how you were today."

"Dumbfounded. I didn't sleep a wink last night, not after witnessing what those fuckers did to Victoria. I don't think I'll ever be able to rid myself of that image, ever. Have you found them yet?"

"Sorry to hear that. Maybe you should visit your GP to ask him for something temporary that will help you to sleep. And no, not yet. We're about to start canvassing your neighbours to see if they either saw or heard anything."

"I saw Gary and Anna last night after you left." He pointed at the house directly next door. "They dropped by to ask how I was. They didn't see anything. They were in the kitchen at the back when the killers struck."

"Do they have any cameras?"

"No. Their doorbell cam is hit and miss. It's been on the blink for a few months. Gary was cursing the fact that he hadn't replaced it by now. One of those things that gets pushed down the to-do list."

"These things happen. We're so reliant on technology these days that when it goes wrong, it can be a pain in the rear. Okay, is there anything you need from us? That is, apart from the obvious."

"No, I don't think so. Will you call me the minute you make the arrest? I don't think I'll be able to sleep properly until those bastards are locked up. What if they come back here? To bump me off?"

"I doubt it. Try and get some rest. You have my word that I'll ring you as soon as we have them in custody, if only to give you some peace of mind."

He waved, too choked to answer, and closed the door slowly.

Fighting her own emotions, Sam returned to the car. "It's really hit him badly. No one should have to see their loved one in that state. I reckon it has scarred him for life. He's going to need professional help to get over it."

"Did you tell him that? Maybe he could see Rhys," Bob suggested.

Sam nodded. "I told him to make an appointment to see his GP. It didn't even occur to me to mention Rhys. I don't like to bring it up too often at work because it always sounds like I'm touting business for him. I'm not. I'm just trying to help."

"I know that. There are four houses here; shall we take two each?"

"Make that three. Gary and Anna, who live in the house next door, called round to see Jason last night. I asked him if they had any cameras; he told me they're on the blink and have been for months."

"That's a bummer. I reckon they would have got a decent angle of the killers as they pulled up. That's what we're after, isn't it? Finding an image of Grace and Harry in the car without their masks on."

"That would be ideal, but whether we get it is a different story. All we can do is our best. Another thing to consider with any images we locate is, ideally, whether we can capture Grace's tattoo on the footage. That would be irrefutable evidence against Grace, at least."

"You're right, we'd definitely have her bang to rights."

They split up and knocked on the remaining houses. One of the neighbours was in, and the other had set off for work early and wouldn't be back until four. Sam left her card with the homeowner she'd spoken to, asking her to pass it on to the missing neighbour so that they could get in touch if they had any footage to offer. The neighbour Sam had spoken to had cameras, but they were angled at their own drive and didn't have the range they were searching for.

Bob, on the other hand, struck lucky. He signalled for Sam to join him when she was free. Terry, the homeowner, was showing him footage on his phone from his house camera, not a doorbell cam. The footage was a lot clearer. They observed the Micra's arrival, noting the two occupants donning masks as they prepared to assault Victoria. However, the image required enhancement for court admissibility.

"Can we get a copy of that? We'll need to get the lab to work their magic on it and see if they can clean up the image for us," Sam asked.

"Of course. Why don't you come in and wait? I've got it linked to my main computer, so I can copy the footage over to a disc for you."

"Brilliant. We really appreciate it."

He showed them through to a study at the rear. He worked swiftly, far quicker than Sam was capable of when dealing with her computer and any of its accessories.

"Let's see. If I hit this button here, it should transfer the footage."

A bar filled to capacity on the screen as the information loaded.

He ejected the disc and slotted it back into the clear plastic case, then handed it to Bob who was the nearest.

"This is fantastic. We can't thank you enough for your help," Sam said as they made their way back up the hallway.

"You're welcome, anything to help. We were all heartbroken to hear what had happened to Vicky. She was a lovely lady. She'd do anything for you. I know journalists can be a bit up themselves, but that wasn't the case with her at all."

"So we've heard. Hopefully, with the footage you've supplied, we'll be able to arrest the killers."

He held up his crossed fingers. "If you do, I think everyone will sleep better in their beds at night. Have you got any indication as to who the killers might be, yet?"

"Let's just say we're following up on a few leads that have come our way today."

"That's great. After speaking with some of the other villagers who live closer to the café, I was told that having you and your team on site has put them at ease."

"That's good news. We're hoping to make an arrest within the next day or two."

"Wow! Let's hope that's the case. Those bastards have caused enough heartache to last a lifetime. Maybe that was their intention."

Sam shrugged. "Who knows what goes through people's heads when they start down this path? Thanks again for your help."

"A pleasure. Good luck."

Sam returned to the car with Bob. "I'm thinking we should get this over to the lab right away. What do you think?"

"If it's a case of waiting around all day for Grace and her mother to come back from shopping, then we'll be better off making ourselves useful in the meantime."

They drove back to Workington and handed the disc to one of the techs. "We could do with the results as soon as you can. We believe we've captured two serial killers on the disc. We need their images enhanced before they put on their masks, and we believe one of them has a large tattoo on their right hand. If we can get proof that it's the suspect we're after who is in the car, there will be no denying the truth."

"Leave it with me. As it happens, I've just completed the job I was on," the male tech said. He leaned in and added, "I'll squeeze yours in next. I shouldn't but... anything to get two serial killers banged up, right?"

Sam smiled. "Thanks, let's hope that's the case. Here's my card. You can call me when it's ready to be picked up. I'll send a member of my team to collect it."

"It should only take me a couple of hours at most. Someone can drop by around two."

"Amazing. Someone will be here then."

Sam and Bob left the lab and drove back to Ennerdale Bridge. The team reported their findings as soon as they arrived. Not long after, Emma brought them a tray of coffee with slices of carrot cake for both of them.

"That's so kind of you. Let me pay you, Emma."

"Nonsense, don't be so insulting. This is on me. I wanted to ask if you'd made any progress yet."

"Nothing definite so far. Bob and I interviewed Victoria's neighbours this morning, and we believe we have uncovered footage that places Grace and Harry at the scene."

Emma appeared puzzled by the news. "I thought you already had that."

"Sorry, yes, we had the make and model of the car, but this new footage shows the killers sitting in the car before they put their masks on."

"Ah, I'm with you now. Do you think it was Grace?"

"It was too far away for us to see. We've whisked it over to the lab. They're going to prioritise it for us; we should hear back in a couple of hours. How are you and Suzy holding up?"

"We're fine. Still shocked by the revelation. Setting that aside, it's the families of the victims that we've got to think about now, isn't it?"

Sam sipped at her much-needed coffee. "It is. They're the ones who will continue to suffer, knowing that the killers are still at large."

"I dread to think what Brenda is going to say about all of this."

"Brenda?" Sam asked, confused. It wasn't a name they had come across during the investigation so far.

"Grace's mum."

"Oh God, don't. What's she like?"

"A wonderful lady, as was her husband. And before today, I would have said Grace had the same genes. Such a loving family. It's appalling to think how much hatred Grace must have coursing through her to go on a murder spree. Do you think it's because of Harry's influence?"

"I don't know; we'll find out more during the interview once we've caught them. I think it will probably have something to do with her father's death. Maybe losing him is what has tipped her over the edge."

"But that was eighteen months ago. Wouldn't she have acted upon it sooner?"

"Possibly. We tend to find that there's usually a trigger behind why family members go on the rampage. We need to find out what that is, as it will be pivotal to the investigation." Sam took a bite of the carrot cake. "Yum, this is delicious."

"All homemade by the wonderful bakers in the village. That's why

I love living here, well, mostly. We have a fabulous community spirit that you'd struggle to find elsewhere."

"It hasn't gone unnoticed, I assure you. Why do you think we prefer to set up base here during an investigation?"

Emma blushed and then left.

"My heart goes out to Emma," Claire said. "She must feel crushed about what's going on."

"She'll be fine once we've caught Grace and punished her and Harry. It's the victims and their families we need to consider. What have you all found out about the couple? Anything of interest?"

"I searched where they were during all three murders, or should I say, in the hours leading up to the murders," Claire said. "And yes, they were definitely together, according to their SM accounts. I'd go as far as to say that Grace even gloated about what she was up to."

"Blatantly?" Sam asked.

"More like in code. I'm going to print off all the information for when it's needed in court."

"That's what I like to hear, PMA, *when* and not if. You'll go far, Claire."

"Get away with you. I'm only doing my job, boss."

"What about the car? Have we nailed who it belongs to yet?"

Oliver raised his hand, and she crossed the room, coffee in hand, to speak with him.

"Go on."

"Claire gave me the address of the owner. I've done some digging of my own and come up with the fact that the Micra belongs to Harry's grandma, Elizabeth Bradley."

"Excellent. Well done, all of you. The only thing left for us to do is obtain the proof from the lab that will be indisputable. Then we can swoop in and make the arrests, hopefully by the end of the day. Let's keep digging. The more evidence we can find relating to where they were at the time of each murder, the better."

Bob sat at the desk beside her. "So, we're going to do a Sidney Youngblood, for now."

"A what?" Sam asked, her brow wrinkling in confusion.

"We're going to sit and wait, sit and wait!"

Sam sighed and ran a hand over her face. "Goodness me, you're really showing your age there, partner."

He grinned. "I'm not. If anything, it's before my time. I happened to hear the catchy tune on the radio on the way in this morning."

"Whatever amuses you."

During the afternoon, Sam tried to keep busy rather than sitting there watching the clock tick by slowly. The team had worked their socks off, and it wasn't until she asked to see the PM result for Grace's father that things finally slotted into place.

"Holy shit balls. This is it; this has to be the trigger: the reason Grace and Harry have sunk to the levels they have."

"Are you talking in riddles again?" Bob said. "What have you found?"

"According to this, Grace's father was murdered. He was a keen hiker who used to go up to Ennerdale Water most days. One day, he went up there late in the evening and didn't come home. It was too dark to search for him. The family went out of their minds with worry until first light. Grace insisted that her mother should stay at home in case her father found his way back to the house. She knew he had intended to go to the upper end of the lake and headed off up that way. She found evidence that someone had lit a small fire on the edge of the woodland... Crap, it was close to the well... where the second victim was found."

"Bugger, how was he killed?" Bob asked. He stepped closer to peer over her shoulder.

"A gang of youths beat him up and left him to die up there... in the well."

"What the fu...? So that's where she got the idea from. Hang on, if that scenario was written about in the book Keane wrote, why the heck didn't she set out to kill him?"

Sam faced her partner and stared at him. "It's been her intention all along to frame Keane. She stole his personal items during the burglary and placed them at the scene of each murder, hoping that we'd automatically suspect Keane. She must be frustrated as hell that we haven't at least pulled him in for questioning. Working here, she's kept on top of the investigation and used it to her advantage to avoid being captured."

"Christ, you couldn't make this up, could you? Well, maybe you could. How irresponsible was it for Keane to use her father's murder as a scene in one of his books?"

Sam exhaled an exasperated breath. "Maybe he didn't intend to."

"Come on, you can't believe that. That murder was carried out exactly as it was written in the manuscript."

"Or think about it: it could have been taken from Grace's memory. Maybe the way her father was killed has haunted her since his death."

Bob shook his head. "I don't think so. Didn't Emma say Grace was part of the book club and they held a Q and A with Keane recently?"

"That's right."

"Well, that's your answer. She must have read about her father's death in the book and set out on her murderous mission."

Sam frowned as his idea expanded in her mind. "So, instead of punishing the person who brought the story to life, she thought she'd kill off the book club members who enjoyed the novel. During the Q and A, they probably fawned all over Keane, and that's what sparked her anger."

"Damn warped if you ask me. If she was the one who broke into Keane's house, why the heck didn't she finish him off and be done with it? Why bring the other victims into this?"

"We could debate this, going round and round in circles for hours, and never get to the real reason behind why she chose the victims over killing Keane himself. What is puzzling me more than anything is the fact that Harry has been a willing participant in this plan."

"Or has he?" Bob said. "What if she's got something over him?"

Sam closed her eyes and heaved out a frustrated sigh.

"They seem besotted with each other, judging by what I've seen on their SM accounts," Claire added. "I can't see him doing anything against his will, but I've been known to be wrong in the past."

"Not often, Claire, you've got great instincts. What can you tell us about Harry and his family? Maybe there's something there."

Claire turned to her screen, and Sam walked over to join her.

"He seems a bright enough lad. He doesn't appear to have many close friends, although he has a fair few on Facebook. But he doesn't tend to post much. Looking back several years to when he joined the site in two thousand, he had a sister who always posted silly memes about him. They dried up around a year later. I've since discovered that she was killed in a hit-and-run accident in Workington. If I had to put money on it, I would say that's when his personality changed."

"That would make sense, especially if they were close. When did he get together with Grace?"

Claire scrolled back through Harry's posts. "Around six months ago."

"And did his character change once more? I'm guessing it did."

"Yes, his posts became much lighter, not so morbid."

"So, that means she had a positive impact on him, at least to start with," Sam said, more to herself than Claire.

"I'd agree. About three months ago, the memes became somewhat darker."

"Okay, let's get all the facts written down and printed off, Claire. So, what we're effectively saying here is that we suspect Grace is the more dominant one in the relationship?"

"I'd say that, yes."

"Thanks." Sam glanced up at the clock on the wall. It was one-thirty—not long to wait now. "Oliver, Liam, are you at a convenient place to take a break?"

"I am," Oliver replied.

"So am I," Liam said. "What do you need, boss?"

"Can you both go to the lab to pick up the results? They should be ready by the time you get there. If there's a delay, then you being on site will gee up the tech."

They both hitched on their jackets and left.

"When they get back, we'll go over the disc and then discuss what surveillance we need to set up. I'm determined to draw this investigation to a conclusion today."

"I agree. It would be great to wrap it up and get back to the station," Bob said.

"I quite like it here," Claire replied.

"I do, too, but then I'm biased," Sam said. She wandered out to the hallway and went to the ladies'.

When she returned, Bob stared at her and said, "Did you hear us in there?"

Her eyes widened. "No, why, what have I missed? Have the boys spotted Grace on the road?"

Bob laughed. "Sorry, I was winding you up. I was going to say we heard you in there, but it has kind of backfired."

She marched over to him and punched his upper arm. "This is a serious situation."

"You don't have to remind me; it's called easing the tension."

"What are you smirking at, Claire? We women are supposed to stick together."

"Sorry, boss. It was quite funny, even if the delivery fell flat. But then, what do you expect when it comes from Bob?"

He folded his arms and scowled. "Charming. I won't bother next time, and no, that's not a threat; it's a promise."

Sam laughed. "Who's winding who up now?"

"Whatever."

Liam and Oliver returned to the office at around two forty-five with the proof they needed to bring Grace and Harry in for questioning.

"Holy crap," Bob said. "You can definitely make out it's them now, and there it is, the distinctive tattoo on her hand. We've got them both by the short and curlies."

"Haven't we? It's amazing how enhanced the images can be in the right hands." Sam was tempted to punch the air, but she restrained herself. "Now all we have to do is find them. Should be a doddle, right?"

"Hmm... that remains to be seen. They've been craftier than foxes up until now."

"Liam and Oliver, why don't you go to Harry's house? Don't make it obvious that you're watching the place. We'll shoot over to Grace's family home to see if there's any movement there. As soon as we spot someone in the house, we'll call you and we can hit both houses at the same time."

"Sounds good to me, boss," Oliver said.

They set off. Sam wished her colleagues good luck when they reached the cars parked on the main road that led into the village.

"I sense we're closing in on them, Bob. What do you think?"

"Call it intuition, but I think they have another card or two up their sleeves, yet."

"Why are we never on the same page?"

"What utter tosh," he said, laughing. "I'm just saying. All right, rather than state the obvious 'gut instinct'—because, let's face it, that's usually your line—I came up with another saying."

"It amounts to the same thing, surely?"

"If you say so. Take the next right here."

Sam did as instructed, then drove until he pointed out the house they were looking for. She darted past it, turned around at the end of the cul-de-sac and parked up fifteen feet from the house, which gave them the perfect view of all the front windows and the front door. She then switched off the engine and got comfortable.

"Should we check in with the boys?" Bob asked, phone in hand.

"Why not?"

He dialled the number. "Liam, it's me. Are you at the location?" He put the phone on speaker.

"Yep. No sign of any vehicles on the drive or parked up outside the house. What about you?"

"All quiet at our end. There's a car outside. I'll get Claire to run the plates. We'll get back to you if the situation changes." Bob ended the call and immediately rang Claire. "Hi, it's me. Can you check a registration for me?"

"Of course."

Bob gave her the details. "Can you ring me back ASAP?"

"Will do."

Bob sank lower into his seat.

Claire rang back a few minutes later. "The car belongs to Brenda Connelly."

Bob sat up and shared a puzzled glance with Sam. "That's the mother's car. Perhaps they've gone shopping in Grace's," Sam said. Her gaze shifted back to the house. She spotted the curtain move at the upstairs window. "Did you see that?"

"No, what did you see?"

"The curtain twitched upstairs. There's someone at home. Come on."

"I'll ring you back, Claire. Wait, Sam, what about Oliver and Liam? You told them we were going to hit the two properties at the same time. Have you changed your mind?"

Sam muttered the worst expletive lingering on the tip of her tongue and came to a stop five feet from the house. She spun around. "Make the call."

He scrolled through his previous calls and picked out Liam's number. "We're going in. We've spotted someone inside. I'll keep the line open."

"Roger that. We're getting out of the car and approaching the house now. Fifteen feet... ten... five... We're ringing the bell."

Bob nodded for Sam to do the same.

"No answer at this end," Liam said.

The door opened, and Sam stared at an older woman who she assumed was Grace's mother. She flashed her warrant card. "Mrs Connelly, I'm DI Sam Cobbs. Is Grace with you?"

"What's the meaning of this visit? No, my daughter isn't here."

"You went shopping together. How long have you been home?"

"I don't have to tell you that!"

"It's important. Either you tell us, or we'll take you down the station for questioning. Bob, call for backup."

"I'm ending the call, Liam. The suspect isn't here."

Sam pushed past Brenda into the hallway and ran through the house checking all the rooms.

"You can't do this. Who do you think you are? I'm going to ring the station, no, I'm going to call my daughter."

"I wouldn't advise you doing that, Mrs Connelly," Sam told her as she descended the stairs. "Where is she?"

With defiance blazing in her eyes, Brenda replied, "Out."

"Where?"

Brenda glared at her and then at Bob, who had appeared behind Sam. "She met up with Harry while we were out and went off with him."

"Shit!" Sam turned and shoved Bob back outside the house. "Ring Suzanne at the station and get this village flooded with officers. I want one here to sit with her. I don't want her contacting Grace."

"It's too late. She's made the call."

Sam spun around and knocked the phone Brenda was using on the floor. "What did you tell her?"

Brenda was shocked and began sobbing. "What's going on? What's Grace done? Why are you treating me like this? As if I'm... I'm a second-class citizen."

"You seriously don't know?"

"Know what?"

Unsure whether to believe her or not, Sam watched Brenda's reaction when she told her the news. "We believe Grace and Harry are the suspects we've been searching for this week with regard to the murders that have happened in the village."

Brenda's legs wobbled, and she fell against the doorframe to her left. "No, this can't be true. I don't believe you."

"It's the truth. We've now obtained all the evidence we need to arrest them. Where are they? Either tell me, or I'll arrest you for being an accessory. I'm not fooling around. Time is of the essence now."

"I don't know. I just rang her, told her you were here, and she hung up on me."

Sam growled and turned her back on the woman. "How long before a team arrives to take over here?"

"They're on their way; about five minutes."

Sam's mobile rang. "DI Sam Cobbs."

"Boss, it's Suzanne. We've had a call from a woman in Ennerdale Bridge. She was frantic. She found her husband lying in a pool of blood in their garden."

"Shit! Give me the address."

Suzanne reeled it off. "There's more. The two culprits got away, but the victim is still alive. An ambulance will be there shortly."

Sam strained her ear and heard a distant siren. "I can hear them. Thanks, Suzanne. I'll be in touch soon." She ended the call and faced Brenda again. "Your daughter and her boyfriend have tried to take yet another life. Where are they? Is there somewhere they like to hang out together?"

"No, I don't think so." The tears ran down Brenda's cheeks.

Sam suspected her emotions were all part of the act. She had no sympathy whatsoever for the woman.

"Sergeant, ring Liam and Oliver. See if they've had any luck over there."

"They haven't, I've just checked. They've searched the back of the house, too."

"Okay. Ask them to join us."

Bob made the call outside the property and then rejoined Sam. By this time, she and Brenda had relocated to the lounge. Brenda had picked up a silver frame and was hugging it.

"Dennis would be turning in his grave if he knew what she's done."

"Was she close to her father?"

"Yes, they were inseparable. Sometimes I felt like an outsider when we were all together."

"I'm sorry to hear that. So, her father's death must have hit her hard then?"

"Of course it did. What a stupid question. I need to see her. Why have you taken my phone from me?"

"I would have thought that was obvious. Why don't you tell us where she is?"

"Read my lips, because I don't bloody know. She doesn't give me an itinerary for every hour she's awake. She's a free spirit; she comes and goes as she pleases."

"Maybe if you had kept a closer eye on her, three residents of this village might still be here today."

"I don't believe she's involved in these heinous crimes. What evidence do you have?"

"I'm not at liberty to reveal that at this time. Where is she?"

Brenda rolled her eyes, frustrated. "With Harry. That's all I know."

Liam and Oliver arrived within minutes.

Sam handed Brenda's phone to Oliver. "Don't let her ring her daughter. They've struck again. Bob and I are going over to check out the victim now. I think he's still alive."

"Thank God. We've got this, boss. Is there a patrol on the way?"

Sam lowered her voice and replied, "We're going to flood the village. They won't escape this time."

She and Bob raced back to the car and drove to the address Suzanne had given them. The ambulance was at the scene. The victim's wife opened the side gate for Sam and Bob to enter.

The woman was in a terrible state. "My husband, please don't let him die."

Sam clutched the woman's hands. "Please, I need you to listen to me. Can you tell me what happened?"

"Two people came in through the gate. They were wearing masks. Cocky shits walked right up to my husband and stabbed him. I was in the kitchen and banged on the window. I don't think they were expecting me to be here. I came tearing out of the kitchen. They dropped a pair of gloves beside my husband and ran off."

"Did you hear them talk to each other? Call each other a name, perhaps?"

"Yes, yes. It sounded like Harry."

"Okay. Thank you. How is your husband doing?"

"They're just taking him to hospital. The paramedic told me they believe the wounds aren't serious, in that the vital organs have been missed." She sighed. "My husband only retired last year. This was supposed to be our time together. To take life easy. He had a very stressful career, and it took him months to get used to the idea of not going to work every day, and now this…"

"What work did your husband do before he retired?"

"He was a pathologist."

Sam's gaze shot to the victim lying on the ground. She could only make out the man's legs. "It's not Richard Evans, is it?"

"Yes, that's right. You probably know him."

"I do." Sam shot across the lawn and crouched beside the victim, keeping out of the way of the paramedics dealing with his wounds. "Richard, it's Sam Cobbs. The paramedics are going to take good care of you."

He raised a hand and whispered, "Sam, is that you? Get the people who did this to me."

"Don't worry, we will. We know who they are. Just keep fighting, Richard, you've got this." She bent and kissed him on the cheek, then she patted the paramedic on the shoulder. "Do your very best for him. He used to be one of us."

"Don't worry, we'll take good care of him."

Sam returned to where Bob was awkwardly comforting Richard's wife. "Can we make you a drink?"

"No. I'll get one at the hospital. I'm hoping they'll allow me to go with them."

"They will. Do you have any children?"

"No. It's just the two of us. Please don't worry about us; I'd rather you go after the people who tried to kill my husband."

"We're on it. We have backup on the way. They won't get away, not this time. Take care. I'll be in touch soon."

They raced back to the car.

"Shit, I've just realised something… Richard was the pathologist who carried out the post-mortem on Grace's father."

"Damn," Bob said. "That's just sick. He was only doing his job, and she's taken umbrage with him."

"Yep. The sooner we arrest these two, the better. Who knows who they'll go after next?"

Sirens sounded all around the village and, as Sam drew up outside The Gather, patrol cars began pulling up at the café.

"Shit, Emma is going to be furious with me. Let's try and keep them out of the car park." Her mobile rang and, talk of the devil, Emma's name popped up on the caller ID screen. "Hi, I know what you're going to say. I'm getting them shifted now."

"Sam, shut up for a minute. I was out collecting eggs, and I've just spotted Grace and Harry. I waved to them, keeping up the pretence that I don't know anything."

"Good girl. Sorry, that sounded condescending. Where were you?"

"I was at the end of Turnpike Road. They took the turning ahead of me. That's the road out to Max's place."

"Shit. Okay, thanks, Emma. Backup has arrived. We'll get them organised. Are you on your way back to TG?"

"Yes, I'm just parking in my usual spot. I can see all the patrol cars in front of me. Tell me they're not going to be here long."

"They're not, I promise. I'm here, too. I'll see you soon. Do you need a hand?"

"I've got a lot of eggs to carry, if you have anyone spare."

"I'll send Bob. Stay where you are. He's on his way."

She grinned at her partner. He grunted, his disapproval evident, and walked down the hill to assist Emma.

Sam clapped to gain the attention of the officers who had exited their vehicles. "I'm going to need you to carefully park your vehicles in the main road. Try around the corner, outside the Fox and Hounds, or down by the church. We need to keep this car park free for the café's customers. Once you've parked, jog back here and join me and my team upstairs. We've set up a temporary office above the café. Make it snappy. We've had a sighting of the killers, and I want to get on it right away."

Bob and Emma appeared, laden with dozens of trays of eggs.

"Thanks for the help, Bob," Emma said. "Are you going after Grace now?"

"Yes, I'm just rallying the troops. We'll be on the way soon. Actually, I'm going to give Max a call to warn him." Sam rang, but the phone went straight to voicemail.

"Damn, I never thought about that," Emma said.

Helen opened the front door for Emma. "I see you've got a charming young man to help you, as usual."

"I try my best," Emma replied.

She was smiling, but Sam knew that deep down her friend was anxious about how the day was going to pan out.

She wasn't alone. Sam was also worried about what lay ahead of them.

The officers ran up the incline towards her. She ushered them upstairs and waited for Bob before she joined them.

"We need to get out to Keane's place, now. We're wasting time," Bob whispered.

"I'm aware of that. The key will be in the planning. We'll be out of here within a few minutes. First, I'm going to send an officer to take over from Liam and Oliver."

"Makes sense."

They ran up the stairs together.

Sam tapped the nearest officer on the shoulder and gave him Brenda's address. "I need you to relieve two members of my team. I want you to watch Brenda Connelly like a hawk. Don't allow her out of your sight, except when she uses the loo. But even then, I need you to ensure she hasn't got a phone with her."

"Yes, ma'am." He bolted down the stairs.

Sam addressed the rest of the officers assembled in front of her, making them aware of the situation and how important it was for them to locate Grace and Harry before they could harm anyone else.

Claire wished Sam luck as she led the team back downstairs and out to their vehicles. "I'll meet you down by the bridge. The road we're going to take can be dangerous in certain sections. Keep your wits about you at all times. Check for a white Nissan Micra en route, just in case they're intent on playing further games with us."

The officers jogged off to collect their cars. Sam left it a few seconds then drove down and waited for them to join her at the bridge. Once all the cars were visible in her mirror, the convoy set off. Sam kept her speed at a steady thirty, not wishing to risk coming a cropper at any of the sharp corners. As the road straightened ahead of them, Bob pointed.

"Shit! I see smoke."

"He's got a wood burner. It'll be the smoke from that."

"I'm telling you, you don't get that much smoke from a wood burner. Put your foot down."

Adrenaline pumping, she squeezed down on the accelerator, finally ignoring the speed limit now that the dangerous bends were behind them. The house came into view through the clearing ahead. That's when she realised Bob was right—it was on fire.

"Call the fire brigade and get an ambulance out here," she shouted and pushed down harder on the accelerator.

Bob made the call. She screeched to a halt in front of the cottage. There was no sign of the Micra.

"Don't tell me they've got away again."

"We haven't passed them on the road. They have to be around here somewhere."

Sam flung the door open and ordered the officers to spread out and search the woodland on either side of the house. Before they began, Sam ensured they all had her phone number.

"Ring me as soon as you spot them. Bob, can you organise a drone?"

He rang the station as they walked towards the property. Sam banged on the front door. There was no answer. She ran around the back to find the door unlocked. Max's cat flew past her the second the door opened.

"Max, Max, are you in here?" She strained an ear to listen but heard nothing, except the roar of the fire in the rooms beyond the kitchen. She dampened a tea towel and covered her hair.

"No, don't go in there, Sam! You can't. It's not safe. It's too far gone."

"I'm going. You stay here."

"I'm coming with you. I refuse to let you tackle this alone." Bob soaked the hand towel hanging up behind the door and wrapped it around his head. He looked like Little Red Riding Hood.

Luckily, they knew the layout of the cottage. Sam tore through the downstairs and into the lounge. Max was lying on the floor, writhing in agony. He had been crucified, large nails driven into his palms, pinning him to the floor. The flames were a few feet away from him. Setting her own safety aside, Sam removed the tea towel, the only defence she had against the flames, and draped it over his face. Bob placed the towel covering his head over Max's body.

"We need to get the nails out. See if you can find any tools we can use, like a claw hammer."

"The fire has taken hold. We're not going to have enough time, Sam."

"Okay, we can delay it. Fill saucepans with water, hurry!"

Bob flew back to the kitchen and returned with two pots of cold water.

"Wet the floor all around him. Hopefully, it'll delay the flames." She shook Max's shoulder. "Max, can you hear me?"

She checked his pulse; it was there but very faint. She and Bob started coughing, the smoke attacking their lungs. She covered her mouth with her hand and went in search of a toolbox. She found a small one under the sink in the kitchen. Her mobile rang; it was Oliver.

She quickly answered it. "Tell me you've got them?"

"We've spotted the car. They've dumped it in the woods. We're on foot, tracking the bastards now. I've put a call in for a K9 team to join us."

"Well done. We've found Max. He's alive but fading fast. We're trying to get him out of here, but the fire is too intense."

"You shouldn't be in there, boss. Do you want me and Liam to come back to give you a hand?"

"Yes, do that. Ensure the others keep up the search. We can't let them get away. The path to the village needs to be cut off. Organise that, Oliver."

"Will do. Hang in there, boss."

Sam ended the call and opened the toolbox. She removed the top layer to reveal the larger tools lying below. She found just what she was looking for, a claw hammer. She had to get Max out of there. It would be a while before the fire brigade got to them.

"I've found this." She handed the hammer to Bob.

"I can't do it, Sam. What if I hurt him?"

"What?" She snatched the hammer back. "Get out of the way; I'll do it myself. We're losing him. My priority is to save his life, not his hands."

Bob stood his ground. "No, okay, I'll do it. I don't want to get sued for ruining his career."

"You won't. Don't be so ridiculous. Do it. We're running out of time." She peered over her shoulder and threw a pan of water at the flames closest to Max's feet. "Come on, Bob, do it!"

He closed his eyes and eased the first nail out of Max's palm. Blood gushed everywhere, hitting Bob full in the face. He wiped it with the towel he'd used to cover Max's body and proceeded to remove the nail from Max's other hand.

"I've done it."

"Let's get him out of here. I'll take his feet. We'll go out the back way."

Oliver and Liam materialised in the doorway and ran forward to help. Sam and Bob allowed them to take over. She hugged her partner, and the four of them bolted for the kitchen. She peered over her shoulder. The flames licked the floor where Max had been spread out seconds before. The relief was palpable, even more so when the lounge ceiling collapsed in front of her.

She caught up with the others and shoved Bob out of the back door. "Quick, we've got to get out. The ceilings are coming down."

"We're safe. Calm down."

She covered her face with her hands and cried, releasing the pent-up emotions that had driven her to save Max's life. "Oh God. We might have all died in there."

Bob wrapped an arm around her shoulder. "But we didn't. Concentrate on the positives."

Sam's phone rang again. She held up her crossed fingers and closed her eyes as she answered it. "DI Cobbs."

"It's PC Titchard, ma'am. We're within touching distance of them. They've gone to ground, but we roughly know where they are."

"Don't lose them. Where are they?"

"At the back of the woods, close to the village."

"There are teams blocking their path from the village side, and the K9 unit is also on the way."

"We'll hold tight until we see movement again."

"Keep me updated." Sam ended the call. "I want to be there when the arrest is made. Liam and Oliver, can you take care of things here? Monitor Keane's condition and wait for the brigade and ambulance to arrive."

"Leave it with us, boss."

"Come on, Bob. We'll head back to the village and approach from that side."

Sam parked up close to the woodland, just behind the other two patrol cars that had been sent ahead. She changed out of her three-inch heels and into her wellies.

"Great. Looks like I'm going to ruin another pair of frigging shoes," Bob grumbled.

"Get some boots and quickly. I'm sick to death of saying the same old thing."

"Sorry. I'll make a note to try harder."

Sam tutted and dug him in the ribs. "Let's go hunting. I hear there are a couple of serial killers within striking distance."

He grinned and gestured for Sam to go ahead of him. "I'm right behind you."

"As usual," she muttered. She began weaving between the saplings that had been planted on the edge of the woodland.

"Dumb question coming up."

"Surprise me," she replied with a groan.

"How do we know we're heading in the right direction? And please, don't tell me you're relying on your gut instinct to guide us."

"Okay, I won't. Umm... next question?"

"You're impossible."

"I know. You should be used to me by now."

"I don't think I'll ever get used to you," he complained.

Sam had already switched her phone to vibrate. It was ringing in her hand. They stopped while she answered it.

"DI Cobbs," she said, keeping her voice low.

"PC Titchard here, ma'am," the officer whispered in response. "They're on the move again."

"Can you close in without them noticing you? We'll do the same from this side. Can you also contact your colleagues who are ahead of us?"

"We'll see what we can do. And yes, I'll call my colleagues to make them aware that you're close behind them and tell them to remain vigilant without advancing towards them."

"Great. Thanks." She ended the call and peered through the trees ahead of them. "Can you see anything? You know what my eyesight is like from a distance."

"Not yet, and it's time you bit the bullet and went to the optician."

She pulled a face and motioned for them to continue but to keep low.

"Easy for you to keep down, you're lower to the ground than I am."

She laughed but then froze. She heard shouting ahead of them. "Quick, we have to get a move on."

"The team in front of us must have broken cover." Bob bolted ahead of her.

Within seconds, she could see three officers, all with Tasers, shouting at Grace and a young man, who Sam assumed was her boyfriend. The officers ordered them to drop the weapons they were holding.

"Screw you," Grace sneered at the officers. "Go on, fire, you ain't got the guts."

Harry's weapon clattered to the ground, and he held up his hands. "Come on, Grace. Do as they say. The game is up."

"Never." Grace wrenched Harry by the arm, drawing him towards her. She held a large kitchen knife to his throat. The tip of the blade nicked his skin, and a trickle of blood dripped onto his T-shirt.

"Grace, what are you doing? We're in this together. Please, don't hurt me."

"I've been using you all along," she screeched in his face.

"What are you talking about? I thought you loved me. What about the future we've planned together?"

Grace let out a crazed laugh. "In your dreams, arsehole. I've got what I wanted. We were drawn together through our misery."

Sam watched every move Grace made and listened to every word she said, with interest. She could tell how bitter and twisted Grace was, and how much she had been disguising her true feelings in order to fulfil her audacious plan. Now, she was standing before them, holding a knife to her partner in crime's throat.

"Come on, Grace, this isn't like you. Put the knife down. Let's talk about this sensibly."

"Piss off. You think you know me, but I've got news for you: you don't. The only person who ever really knew me was my father. He was stolen from me eighteen months ago."

"We understand how traumatic it must have been for you, and seeing your father's death portrayed in a novel must have been shocking to read."

"He had no right to do that. Keane couldn't have given a stuff about the damage he would cause to Mum and me. It was all about how profitable the story could be for him. It sickens me that he should use my father's death to gain notoriety. He was reasonably unknown until that book came out."

"I totally understand how upsetting all of this must have been for you. Come on, let Harry go, and we'll discuss where we go from here. This needn't be the end, Grace."

"Bollocks. It's too late for talking. That's why I set out on the journey and dragged Harry along with me. He was gullible, weren't you?" She tipped his head back, further exposing it to the blade.

Sam raised a hand and took a step closer. "Grace, don't do this. We can get you the help you need to cope with the loss of your father without you killing someone else."

"Do you think I'm stupid? Like the others who have dealt with me over my loss? Well, the one doctor who insisted I should take antidepressants to see me over the bad time, as he put it. Mum might like popping pills day in and day out, but it's not for me. People grieving in this community are shoved aside and told they just have to get on with it. If only it were that simple. My father was my rock. He was there for me one day and gone the next. His life was snuffed out by that gang of youths who thought it would be fun to crush his legs and throw him in a well, leaving him to die. Can you imagine the pain, the torment he went through in the hours leading up to his death?"

"No, I can't begin to imagine how scared and vulnerable he must have felt. In order for you to heal, Grace, you need to look past that and remember all the good times you shared with your father. It's the only way you can keep his memory alive."

Grace's expression changed for a fleeting moment until she remembered where she was. That proved to Sam that if she chipped away at her enough, Grace was likely to get distracted, allowing the team to make a move on her.

"Seriously, how do you think your father would react to you holding a knife to Harry's throat now?"

Her head bowed slightly. "He'd be livid... but he'd understand after what I've been through. How I've been left to cope with my loss."

"I can help you get all the help you need to get through this, Grace. Give me the opportunity to do that. Work with me. Release Harry, and we can make a start today."

"How? This is another trick, isn't it? You think that by saying the right thing, I'll drop my guard and you'll be able to take advantage of me. That's all people do in society today—take advantage of those around them without considering what they might be going through. I no longer want to live like that. I'd much rather go out in a blaze of glory. All I've ever wanted was to be by my father's side. He was my world. I miss him every second I'm awake. To have him stolen from me in such a wicked way will haunt me forever."

"Grace, please, let me go," Harry pleaded. "I'm not like the others. You know I'm not. We're partners, you and me against the world."

"We've never been that. Why can't you get it into that thick head of yours that you were a mere pawn in my game? A useless prick most of the time, who frustrated the hell out of me. I played along, letting you believe you were in charge, all the time laughing at the stupid mistakes you made along the way. If it had been down to you, none of the victims would have been murdered, would they? You wanted to keep them alive, too scared to end their lives when it came down to it."

"It wasn't like that. Some of the victims I knew. We should have stuck with my idea in the first place and punished Keane instead. But you refused to listen to me. You came up with the plan to frame him for the murders. The poor bloke is a recluse. Everyone in the village knows he never leaves the house. How the heck could he have committed the murders? You didn't think any of this through, not really. I warned you we'd get caught. I begged you to stop after the first murder, but by then, you'd got a thirst for it, hadn't you? You were determined to kill them. Nothing I could have said would have stopped you. Why didn't you listen to me? If you had, we wouldn't be in this mess today."

A grin spread Grace's lips apart, revealing her straight white teeth. She kissed Harry on the forehead and slit his throat before those around her had the chance to stop her.

She held the knife in the air, then angled it towards her chest.

"Do it!" Sam shouted.

An officer Tasered Grace before she could turn the knife on herself. She dropped to her knees. Sam and Bob ran to see if they could help Harry, but it was too late. Fortunately for him, his life had ended quickly. Grace had used so much force making the cut that she'd nearly decapitated him in the process.

The Taser wires were removed from Grace's chest, and she was hoisted to her feet by two officers.

Sam stood in front of her and shook her head. "You should have sought help before robbing other people of their lives. You're an evil individual who deserves to spend the rest of your life in prison. I doubt if you've even considered what your selfish behaviour would do to your mother, have you?"

"She doesn't care about me. All she's interested in is spending the insurance money she received after Dad's death."

"I think you're deluded if you believe that. Your mother loves you very much. You were too wrapped up in your own selfish behaviour to notice it. Get her out of my sight."

Grace snarled and spat at Sam. The saliva fell short and landed on the leaves in front of her. Sam smiled and said nothing.

I'll get my day in court against you, young lady. We'll see who has the last laugh then.

Grace tried to fight the officers restraining her. The cuffs were slapped on her wrists. She shouted expletive after expletive and started kicking out at the officers.

Sam had to step in and tell her to calm down. "You're not doing yourself any favours, Grace. Carry on, and your behaviour will end up going against you in court."

"I don't give a toss." She spat again. "Do your worst, bitch. Maybe if you had investigated the case properly, fewer victims would have been killed. Have you considered that?"

"Get her out of my sight."

"One question. Did he die before you got to him?"

"If you're talking about Max Keane. No, he made it. So, your plan to finish him off failed."

Grace's eyes narrowed, and she attempted to get to Sam, but the officers ended up dragging her back to their car.

"Are you okay?" Bob asked.

"Is she right? Could we have saved at least one or two of the victims?"

"She's just striking out, planting doubts in your mind. You, no *we,* caught the killers in less than a week. That's probably what has got to her."

Sam approached Harry's body and stared down at it. "What a waste. He left this life knowing she had used him. That's what I'm struggling to get my head around: Grace duped so many people." She gasped and faced Bob. "I need to tell Emma before she hears it from anyone else."

"Maybe you should give her a call. I'll ring Des if you want?"

"Thanks, Bob." She walked away from him and rang Emma's mobile. "Emma, it's me. We've caught Grace. I wanted you to hear it from me before the gossip filtered back to you."

"I don't know how I feel about the news, Sam. I should feel elated, but the overwhelming emotion is that of sadness."

"Umm… there's more. We were closing in on them, and I think Grace must have felt cornered. She did something none of us expected. She took Harry hostage and held a knife to his throat."

"It gets worse. I hope you managed to talk her out of doing anything rash."

"Sadly not. She killed him—slit his throat just a few feet in front of us."

"Oh, Sam. That's dreadful. I didn't really know her at all. I would never have thought it possible for her to sink that low. Her poor mother is going to be mortified, especially after losing her husband not long ago. Does Brenda know?"

Sam sighed. "No. I'm going to tell her now before the news gets out. Mind you, I should inform Harry's parents first. Do you know them?"

"They split up years ago. He lives with his father. I think he works away a lot, and Harry used to visit his grandmother regularly."

"That's who owns the Micra. The car they used to get to the crime scenes."

"Oh gosh, I feel sorry for her. She's going to be traumatised to hear the news. You've still got a lot to do... No, what am I thinking? What about Max? Did they get to him? We keep hearing more and more sirens throughout the village."

"They set fire to his house. I shouldn't be telling you this. I'm trusting you not to tell anyone."

"You have my word, Sam. Is Max alive?"

"Yes. They crucified him on the floor. Pierced his hands with four-inch nails."

"What the hell? That's just sick. What on earth was Grace thinking, subjecting the poor man to that?"

"Makes you wonder, doesn't it? The main thing is he's alive. Whether he'll be able to use his hands again is another story. It'll probably take dozens of operations and months and months of rehabilitation to repair the damage."

"She got to him and punished him in the end then."

"She did that all right. I'd better go. I'll see you later."

"Thanks for letting me know."

Sam ended the call then rang Claire back at the office. She informed her about what had taken place and asked Claire to ring the victims' families to let them know that the killers had been, in Grace's case, arrested. She told Claire to keep the news about Harry out of the conversation.

"How did you get on?" she asked Bob once he'd finished his call.

"They're on their way. We don't have to hang around out here, do we?"

"No. We'll get some officers to cordon off the scene and keep an eye on the area until Des gets here."

They picked their way back through the trees to the main road. A patrol car was parked up, and two officers were leaning against the bonnet. Sam instructed them to prepare the site for Des and his team. Then, she drove through the village to the address they had for the grandmother.

Mrs Dalkins greeted them with a frown as she opened the door. "What can I do for you?"

"Sorry to disturb you. We need to come in and have a chat with you about Harry," Sam said.

"Come through to the lounge."

They removed their shoes at the front door and followed the elderly woman into the lounge. She sat in the chair close to the fire and placed a rug over her legs, despite it being quite a warm day.

"I feel the cold most days," she explained. "What does your visit have to do with my grandson?"

"It is with regret that we have to tell you that your grandson died earlier."

"I don't understand. Died? He can't have. You must have made a mistake. He's out with Grace, or that's what he told me. Did they have an accident?"

Avoiding her question, Sam asked, "Are you aware of the deaths that have taken place in the village this week?"

"I've heard the odd rumour from people I've met in the street on my way up to the café for lunch. What does that have to do with my grandson?"

"Harry and Grace killed the victims."

Mrs Dalkins shook her head. "I don't believe you. Harry isn't evil. He wouldn't do such a thing. He's a good lad, sometimes misunderstood, especially by his parents, but he's recently turned a corner. He's been applying for more jobs and... no, this can't be true."

Sam nodded. "I'm sorry, it's true. We caught them in the woods. They'd just set fire to a property owned by a local author. When we confronted them, Grace held Harry hostage and... before we could stop her, she killed him."

The tears flowed, and she plucked a tissue from the box next to her. "Oh my God. What am I going to tell his parents?"

"I can do that for you, if you'd prefer. I'm so sorry for your loss."

"Killers? They killed those people? But why?"

"It appears to have stemmed back from when Grace's father was killed. I've yet to get to the bottom of it. I'm on my way back to the station now to interview her. I wanted to tell you what had happened to Harry before I headed back to Workington. Do you want me to ring Harry's parents?"

"I'll get their phone numbers. I don't think I've got it in me to do it."

Mrs Dalkins left the room and returned with a small notebook a few moments later. "I still can't believe he's gone." She flicked through the pages, and Sam jotted down the numbers for Harry's parents. "They're going to be dumbfounded."

"I know. It's better if they hear the news from me than learn about it on the TV or radio, later. The village is already flooded with journalists looking for a new angle regarding the murders."

"No, that's not right."

"Our hands are tied. We can't stop them reporting. Are you going to be all right?"

"Do you want the honest answer? I don't know."

"Do you want me to call a friend or neighbour to come and sit with you?"

"No. I just need some peace and quiet to allow it to sink in."

Sam rose from her seat and patted the back of Mrs Dalkins' hand. "We'll leave you to it, then. So sorry for your loss."

"Are you? After him killing those people? I feel numb. I'm not sure how I'm going to process it."

"I completely understand. You stay there; we'll let ourselves out."

THE REST of the afternoon was frantic for Sam. After returning to their temporary office, she rang Harry's parents. She wouldn't usually inform a relative of someone's passing over the phone, but as she'd told Harry's grandmother, with the number of journalists hanging around the village, she felt it was important to contact them before a tactless journalist did. His parents reacted as any parent would if they found themselves in the same situation. A gamut of emotions was unleashed on Sam, but she set that aside to complete the task of packing up their temporary base. With everything transferred to the vans Bob had organised, Sam ventured back to the café to say farewell to Emma and her team. The staff were cleaning up, as all the customers had left for the day.

"It's been wonderful seeing you all again. I'm just sorry it was under such difficult circumstances."

Emma took a step forward and hugged her. "It's always good seeing you, Sam. What will happen to Grace now?"

"I'm going back to the station to interview her. If she talks, then fine. If she doesn't, then she'll be sent to the remand centre to await her trial. The evidence is mounting against her. She'd be foolish to deny her involvement in the murders."

"I'm just so... I suppose *disappointed* would be the wrong word here, but you know what I mean. She fooled all of us into believing she was a kind, caring soul, when all the time she was plotting to kill. We've all been discussing it, thankful that she never felt the need to vent her anger on one of us."

"I genuinely believe losing her father has left her confused and bewildered. It's such a shame that Harry got involved with her plans. All he did was try to please her. He was desperate to have a future with her."

"Heartbreaking. What would possess her to end his life like that, knowing what they had 'achieved together'?"

"Who truly knows what goes through serial killers' heads when they're 'in the zone'? Anyway, I wanted to thank you all for looking after us so well this week. I'll see you soon. Maybe at the weekend, if I can twist Rhys' arm to venture down this way for a walk with the dogs."

"We'd love to see you all. Take care, Sam."

She left the café and jumped into her car. They drove back to Workington in a convoy, with Sam at the front of the motorcade.

The desk sergeant, Nick, greeted her with a smile. "Congratulations, ma'am. She's a feisty one. Still kicking off in her cell."

"I thought she might. Okay, I'm going to leave it until the morning to interview her. Maybe she'll be more open to talking to us, then."

"I'd say that was a wise choice."

At the end of their shift, the team met across the road at the pub for a swift drink. Sam's heart really wasn't in it. She was exhausted. All she wanted to do was go home and put her feet up for the evening with Rhys and the boys.

When she finally got home at close to seven, Rhys had cooked them one of his special chillis, which was a welcome treat. "You shouldn't have, but I'm mighty glad you did."

She walked into his open arms. "You look dead on your feet."

"I am, and it's not over yet. I still have to interview the suspect in the morning. I'm not looking forward to that one. Still, I'd rather set work aside for the rest of the evening. Can we eat this, then take the boys for a walk?"

"We can do whatever you want."

They shared a kiss and then sat down to enjoy their meal. Afterwards, Sam loaded the dishwasher they rarely used, and they set off for the park with the dogs. The evening was warm, and the leisurely stroll helped her unwind, to the extent that she pushed aside any thoughts of the investigation when they returned home an hour later.

EPILOGUE

The next morning, Sam made a point of travelling to Whitehaven first thing. She wanted to check on Max personally, to ensure he didn't feel they were neglecting him now that he was in hospital.

"How are you doing, Max?"

"Relieved. Who wouldn't be, knowing that the serial killer I helped to create is behind bars?"

Sam shook her head. "You mustn't think like that, Max. Yes, it was unfortunate that you chose to use her father's murder in your latest bestseller. However, you're not to blame for her going on a killing spree with her boyfriend."

He cringed. "I heard what happened to him. She must be mentally unstable to have killed her accomplice in such a brutal way."

Sam wagged her finger. "I'd rather not go down that route; otherwise, we won't get the trial we want, she'd be sent for a medical assessment instead."

"Tough to know what to do for the best." He stared down at his bandaged hands.

"What's the prognosis? Or is it too early to tell?"

"The surgeon had a word with me last night while he was still on duty. They X-rayed my hands and, according to what he saw, he believes the damage will be minimal, only because the nails used were very slim."

Sam shuddered. "I'm sorry they put you through such an horrendous ordeal."

"It's not your fault, Sam. I don't think I'll be writing any bestsellers for a while. Luckily my hands are insured."

"That's fortunate. I'll keep in touch. I need to get back to the station to interview Grace."

"Good luck with that. Tell her I don't hold her responsible. I should never have used her father's death. It was lazy of me, and I will regret using it until the day I die."

"I'm sorry. I'm not going to tell her that. She was in the wrong, *not* you."

"But it was my reckless actions that tipped her over the edge. I'm not sure if I'll ever be able to forgive myself."

"You will. In time. Wishing you a speedy recovery, Max."

WHEN SAM ARRIVED at the station, she learned that Grace had struck two officers when they had served her breakfast. The duty doctor needed to sedate her, which meant the interview had to be postponed until the afternoon. In the meantime, the team worked hard to collect all the evidence they had, and Sam filled out the necessary paperwork in her office to put the investigation to bed, as far as they were concerned.

Bob knocked on the door at around two. "Hi, I thought you might need reminding what the time is."

She peeked at her watch. "Damn, time flies when you're having fun, apparently. Have you checked how she is?"

"Yep. Nick said she's eager to talk to us."

"Is she? Or is this her playing another one of her games?"

"I guess we're going to find out soon enough."

"I'll be five minutes maximum, here. Can you make the arrangements?"

Sam and Bob entered the interview room to find a dishevelled-looking Grace sitting next to the duty solicitor.

"Are you ready for us?" Sam asked the solicitor, whom she hadn't met before.

"We are. I'm Tina Askew."

Sam and Bob took their seats, then Bob got the recording underway.

"How are you, Grace?"

"All right."

"Are you willing to talk to us?"

"I wouldn't say that. I'm sick of sitting in that cell, so what's the alternative?"

"Then we'll begin. Perhaps you can tell us why you killed Angel Pritchard?"

Grace's gaze met Sam's, and she smirked. "No comment."

Unfortunately, that's how the rest of the interview went. It ended up being a frustrating hour for Sam until she finally asked the male officer at the rear of the room to take her back to her cell.

"You can't hold me here. I know my rights," Grace shouted at the door.

"You think you know your rights. You'll be transferred to the remand centre later today. We've got all the evidence and witness statements we need to bang you up. I doubt if you will ever be set free. I hope it was worth it, Grace."

"It was. I have nothing left in this life, anyway."

The officer led her down the corridor back to her cell.

Sam escorted the solicitor to the reception area, then climbed the stairs with Bob. "Who knew someone could carry that much hatred within them? She has no intention of showing any remorse."

"Maybe a long spell behind bars will change that eventually." Sam shook her head. "I doubt if that's true in her case."

THE END

THANK you for reading To Hurt Them, the next thrilling adventure is The Truth Will Out.

WHILE YOU'RE WAITING for that to come out, have you read any of my other fast-paced crime thrillers yet?

WHY NOT TRY the first book in the DI Sara Ramsey series
   No Right To Kill

OR GRAB the first book in the bestselling, award-winning, Justice series here, Cruel Justice

OR THE FIRST book in the spin-off Justice Again series,
   Gone in Seconds

PERHAPS YOU'D PREFER to try one of my other police procedural series, the DI Kayli Bright series which begins with
   The Missing Children

OR MAYBE YOU'D enjoy the DI Sally Parker series set in Norfolk,

Wrong Place

OR MY GRITTY police procedural starring DI Nelson set in Manchester, Torn Apart

OR MAYBE YOU'D like to try one of my successful psychological thrillers I know The Truth or She's Gone or Shattered Lives

ALSO BY M A COMLEY

Blind Justice (Novella)

Cruel Justice (Book #1)

Mortal Justice (Novella)

Impeding Justice (Book #2)

Final Justice (Book #3)

Foul Justice (Book #4)

Guaranteed Justice (Book #5)

Ultimate Justice (Book #6)

Virtual Justice (Book #7)

Hostile Justice (Book #8)

Tortured Justice (Book #9)

Rough Justice (Book #10)

Dubious Justice (Book #11)

Calculated Justice (Book #12)

Twisted Justice (Book #13)

Justice at Christmas (Short Story)

Prime Justice (Book #14)

Heroic Justice (Book #15)

Shameful Justice (Book #16)

Immoral Justice (Book #17)

Toxic Justice (Book #18)

Overdue Justice (Book #19)

Unfair Justice (a 10,000 word short story)

Irrational Justice (a 10,000 word short story)

Seeking Justice (a 15,000 word novella)

Caring For Justice (a 24,000 word novella)

Savage Justice (a 17,000 word novella)

Justice at Christmas #2 (a 15,000 word novella)

Gone in Seconds (Justice Again series #1)

Ultimate Dilemma (Justice Again series #2)

Shot of Silence (Justice Again series #3)

Taste of Fury (Justice Again series #4)

Crying Shame (Justice Again series #5)

See No Evil (Justice Again series #6)

To Die For (DI Sam Cobbs #1)

To Silence Them (DI Sam Cobbs #2)

To Make Them Pay (DI Sam Cobbs #3)

To Prove Fatal (DI Sam Cobbs #4)

To Condemn Them (DI Sam Cobbs #5)

To Punish Them (DI Sam Cobbs #6)

To Entice Them (DI Sam Cobbs #7)

To Control Them (DI Sam Cobbs #8)

To Endanger Lives (DI Sam Cobbs #9)

To Hold Responsible (DI Sam Cobbs #10)

To Catch a Killer (DI Sam Cobbs #11)

To Believe the Truth (DI Sam Cobbs #12)

To Blame Them (DI Sam Cobbs 13)

To Judge Them (DI Sam Cobbs #14)

To Fear Him (DI Sam Cobbs #15)

To Deceive Them (DI Sam Cobbs #16)

To Hurt Them (DI Sam Cobbs #17)

The Truth Will Out (DI Sam Cobbs #18)

Forever Watching You (DI Miranda Carr thriller)

Wrong Place (DI Sally Parker thriller #1)

No Hiding Place (DI Sally Parker thriller #2)
Cold Case (DI Sally Parker thriller #3)
Deadly Encounter (DI Sally Parker thriller #4)
Lost Innocence (DI Sally Parker thriller #5)
Goodbye My Precious Child (DI Sally Parker #6)
The Missing Wife (DI Sally Parker #7)
Truth or Dare (DI Sally Parker #8)
Where Did She Go? (DI Sally Parker #9)
Sinner (DI Sally Parker #10)
The Good Die Young (DI Sally Parker #11)
Coping Without You (DI Sally Parker #12)
Could It Be Him (DI Sally Parker #13)
Frozen In Time (DI Sally Parker #14)
Echoes of Silence (DI Sally Parker #15)
The Final Betrayal (DI Sally Parker #16)
Garden of Bones (DI Sally Parker #17)
Web of Deceit (DI Sally Parker Novella)
The Missing Children (DI Kayli Bright #1)
Killer On The Run (DI Kayli Bright #2)
Hidden Agenda (DI Kayli Bright #3)
Murderous Betrayal (Kayli Bright #4)
Dying Breath (Kayli Bright #5)
Taken (DI Kayli Bright #6)
The Hostage Takers (DI Kayli Bright Novella)
No Right to Kill (DI Sara Ramsey #1)
Killer Blow (DI Sara Ramsey #2)
The Dead Can't Speak (DI Sara Ramsey #3)
Deluded (DI Sara Ramsey #4)
The Murder Pact (DI Sara Ramsey #5)

Twisted Revenge (DI Sara Ramsey #6)

The Lies She Told (DI Sara Ramsey #7)

For The Love Of... (DI Sara Ramsey #8)

Run for Your Life (DI Sara Ramsey #9)

Cold Mercy (DI Sara Ramsey #10)

Sign of Evil (DI Sara Ramsey #11)

Indefensible (DI Sara Ramsey #12)

Locked Away (DI Sara Ramsey #13)

I Can See You (DI Sara Ramsey #14)

The Kill List (DI Sara Ramsey #15)

Crossing The Line (DI Sara Ramsey #16)

Time to Kill (DI Sara Ramsey #17)

Deadly Passion (DI Sara Ramsey #18)

Son of the Dead (DI Sara Ramsey #19)

Evil Intent (DI Sara Ramsey #20)

The Games People Play (DI Sara Ramsey #21)

Revenge Streak (DI Sara Ramsey #22)

Seeking Retribution (DI Sara Ramsey #23)

Gone... But Where? (DI Sara Ramsey #24)

Last Man Standing (DI Sara Ramsey #25)

Vanished (DI Sara Ramsey #26)

Shadows of Deception (DI Sara Ramsey #27)

The Killing Route (DI Sara Ramsey #28)

I Know The Truth (A Psychological thriller)

She's Gone (A psychological thriller)

Shattered Lives (A psychological thriller)

Evil In Disguise – a novel based on True events

Deadly Act (Hero series novella)

Torn Apart (Hero series #1)

End Result (Hero series #2)

In Plain Sight (Hero Series #3)

Double Jeopardy (Hero Series #4)

Criminal Actions (Hero Series #5)

Regrets Mean Nothing (Hero series #6)

Prowlers (Di Hero Series #7)

Sole Intention (Intention series #1)

Grave Intention (Intention series #2)

Devious Intention (Intention #3)

Cozy mysteries

Murder at the Wedding

Murder at the Hotel

Murder by the Sea

Death on the Coast

Death By Association

Merry Widow (A Lorne Simpkins short story)

It's A Dog's Life (A Lorne Simpkins short story)

A Time To Heal (A Sweet Romance)

A Time For Change (A Sweet Romance)

High Spirits

The Temptation series (Romantic Suspense/New Adult Novellas)

Past Temptation

Lost Temptation

Clever Deception (co-written by Linda S Prather)

Tragic Deception (co-written by Linda S Prather)

Sinful Deception (co-written by Linda S Prather)

KEEP IN TOUCH WITH M A COMLEY

Newsletter
http://smarturl.it/8jtcvv

BookBub
www.bookbub.com/authors/m-a-comley

Blog
http://melcomley.blogspot.com

Facebook Readers' Page
https://www.facebook.com/groups/2498593423507951

TikTok
https://www.tiktok.com/@melcomley

Printed in Great Britain
by Amazon